Luke

EMERSON WOLVES BOOK 2

KATHI S. BARTON

WCP

World Castle Publishing, LLC
Pensacola, Florida

Copyright © Kathi S. Barton 2014
Print ISBN: 9781629891682
eBook ISBN: 9781629891699
First Edition World Castle Publishing, LLC, November 7, 2014
http://www.worldcastlepublishing.com

Licensing Notes

Cover: Karen Fuller
Editor: Eric Johnston
Editor: Maxine Bringenberg

Chapter 1

Allen was in Luke's office when Luke came into the room. He watched Allen for several seconds while he fussed with the new desk, then the chair. He looked up when Luke cleared his throat.

"If you sit in my chair before I do, Slone might be a little pissed. She has it in her head that I should use everything first." Allen backed away from the chair like it was going to attack him. "I was kidding, Allen. If you sat in it, no one would care at all."

"I would." Allen moved back as Luke came fully into the room. He sat down and looked at the impressive desk that Slone and Hunter had purchased for him when he took the job as mayor. "It's really nice. She has excellent taste."

"She does at that. I wonder where you'd even get a desk this big. I mean, I thought they made them sort of streamline nowadays. This looks like something that might have come from an old estate or something."

"It's not new. I mean, I don't think it is. The guys who brought it in said that they'd picked it up from a warehouse in Maine and brought it down. Along with a few other items for Mrs. Emerson. She must really like antiques. But one of them mentioned that it came from her own home. He said the place was filled with them." Luke nodded and ran his hands over the smooth oak surface. "I have two appointments for you today, sir. I thought to ease you into this slowly. The first one is with the chief of police, Mr. Granger. He is…I don't think he's happy with the turn of events."

"He can fuck the hell off." Luke leaned back in his equally wonderful chair and asked Allen to have a seat. He sat down, but he didn't look happy about it. "Tell me what you know about him. And so you know, I don't want you to keep things from me. If you know something, anything that might help me make this a better town, I want to know."

"I can do that." He got up and went to the outer office, then returned with a thick notebook. "I have taken notes on everything when the other man was in office. I know that sounds paranoid, but in this business, it's better to have your ass covered than not. I have this in my desk drawers as well as on a thumb drive if you ever want to look at it. I will give you a copy of it weekly if you would like."

"I would. And so you know as well, we've had you investigated." Allen paled before nodding. "I know that you were arrested about four years ago for not having a license or insurance. Also the little problems with the drugs and how that got you put into jail. But we can see that you've reinvented yourself, became a better man. I want you to know that while I want to know these things, I have no intentions of holding them against you. You paid for what you did and you have been an immaculate citizen since. But you fuck up again, and I will take you to the cleaners. Understood?"

"Yes, sir. I didn't disclose it before because I knew that I'd be fired. Or worse yet, targeted by the former mayor. I had in here to tell you first thing." Allen handed him an envelope and stood up. "I've lied to this office, and I know that the consequences for that is termination. There is my —"

"Sit down." Allen sat, perched on the edge of his chair, and Luke pulled out the paper. Just as he'd thought, it was Allen's resignation. Luke put it on the desk and looked at him. "Do you want to quit?"

"No, sir. But I did lie to you and all the others. I have been entrusted with this job to uphold the laws, and I know that breaking them is a terminable offense." Allen stood again, and Luke pointed to the chair until he sat again. "You need to fire me, sir. If word gets out that you kept me on after this, there will be hell to pay from the others."

"You let me worry about them. And you're not leaving. No matter what." Allen looked unsure, but Luke decided that Allen was definitely going to be a part of his team. "These meetings today, who else is coming in and what do I need to know about them?"

Luke picked up the resignation and tore it in half. Then he dropped it in the trash can. Allen sat there for several seconds before Luke said his name again. The poor man looked ready to cry, but pulled open his small computer and began to speak.

"Mr. Osborne will be coming in after lunch. He is the contractor that owns the city contracts to do repairs. I have enclosed in his file a list of the projects he's working on. Or at least ones that he's supposed to be working on. Most of them are unfinished and have been for a long time."

Luke pulled them out and looked them over for a few minutes. "Can you find out the start date of each of these projects and the amount of work that is complete to date?" Allen said he could. "Good. And can you get them to me — not all, because it looks like there are more than a dozen of them, but at least the most current ones — by the time he gets here?"

"I can. Most of the work is incomplete, as I've said before. I walk by two of the projects he's been working on daily and to be honest, I've never seen a single man working. They're there, but they seem to be enjoying the outdoors and their meals much more than they seem to be working. Not to be pointing fingers either, but most of them are drinking on the job. That is a violation of the rules of the contract as well." Allen flushed. "But then, I don't know a great deal about construction sites."

"You know more than you think. And I want you to stop undermining yourself as well. When you have an opinion, it's fine. I might not have the same one, but that doesn't mean it's not valued." Luke looked over three more of the contracts for business and then at Allen. "Can you get my brother Ellis on the phone for me? I think he has his cell, but I left mine at the house. It was dead anyway. "

"Of course." He left and returned in less than a minute. "He's on line two. And he said that he has your phone and is bringing it to you. Would you like for me to set up a conference room for you two to talk?"

"Please." Luke picked up the phone and hit the button. Before he spoke to Ellis, he finished with Allen. "Also, I need for you to get me all you can find out about Osborne and his construction company. Personal as well. See if you can find out when the man comes to work — if he does—and when he leaves for the day. I think Slone mentioned there was a workmen clause in his contract with her."

Allen left the room, and Luke turned to the phone. Ellis was laughing when he said his name. It took Ellis a good two minutes to be able to tell him what was so fucking funny. The man was going to make him beat the shit out of him if he kept this up.

"You. Big bad mayor is ordering people around like he knows what the fuck he's doing. I suppose next thing, you're going to be trying to order me around. Won't work, in case you're wondering. I know your deepest secrets." And Luke knew his. "I have your phone. I charged it on my way in."

"Thank you very much and right now, I hate you." Luke laughed before getting to the point. "Can you do me a favor? There's a building on Main that has been under construction for nearly nine months. I have an address, and if it's the one that I think it is, it should be a good deal further along than it is. I saw trucks there once in all the time we've been here, and there is some concrete poured, but little else." He gave him the address, but Ellis told him he already knew the place.

"I can see it now. I'm parked in front of it. And you're right. Walls should be up, and there should be some windows in place. All they have is a footer poured and some beams lying about. Does it say how big this place is supposed to be?" Luke looked over the contract and told him. "The form isn't nearly big enough for those dimensions...not nearly so. Not unless they're planning to build it about fifty stories high to accommodate the square footage. As it stands now, this thing is smaller than Slone's shed. The bigger one."

Luke looked over the rest of the contract and his brother laughed suddenly. He was almost afraid to find out. "What's going on now? Please tell me that someone has finally showed up to work and is right now doing something to the thing."

"Nope. But a guy with Osborne Construction printed on the side of his truck has just pulled up and he's coming toward me. Could be he wants my advice on how to get this thing started, but I don't think it's going to be that simple. He looks a little high if you ask me. Wait. Yeah, he's high. I can smell it on him. Hang on."

As Luke waited he stood up and looked out his front window. It happened to look out over the main street, and he could just make out his brother's truck. The sign blazing across it was a gift from Slone last night, and it proclaimed Emerson Construction as the best in the state. He doubted that was true, but it certainly looked like it in comparison to the other crew in this town.

The guy from Osborne's stepped back from Ellis's truck when the door opened. His brother was getting out, it seemed.

It was over almost as soon as it began. The guy took a swing at Ellis, and Ellis ducked. When he came back up, the other man was sailing across the road and hit his parked truck with his body. The truck was one of those nice big suckers, but it didn't stand a chance against a powerful wolf like his brother was. Luke shouted for Allen to call the police. In seconds, less time than he thought it should have taken, the cruiser pulled up and they shoved Ellis against his truck. Luke left his office to go to his brother.

By the time he was outside, Ellis was being cuffed. The other man was being helped up and someone was treating his wounds. Luke stood in front of the cruiser door and asked them what the hell they were doing. They'd either answer him or stand there all day for all he cared.

"He assaulted this man, and in case you didn't know it, that's a crime here abouts. There was no cause for it, as Danny here was just walking down the sidewalk and Emerson here attacked him. What kind of pervert does shit like that? Your kind I guess." Luke looked at the injured man, then at the cop who continued talking to him in the same, I'm-better-than-you sort of tone. "You might want to stand back there, Mayor, before I have to arrest you too for obstructing justice."

"I have no idea what you mean by my kind, but I'll have to assume you mean upstanding citizens. But I want you to also know that I saw the whole thing. That man was the first person to swing. My brother was just defending himself." The cop just chuckled. "You think this is funny? You do know that I can have you arrested for false imprisonment, don't you?"

"I've not put him in prison as yet. I'm only taking him downtown to cool off in one of the cells. If you want to come and bail him out, you be my guest. But I have to tell you now, you'll need to bring a lot of cash. Your kind…well, we don't take checks from animals."

Luke felt his wolf run along his skin. The cop must have felt it too because he took a step back before he crossed his arms over his chest and glared. Luke turned to his brother, and when he nodded, Luke turned back. He had a sudden idea.

"You're fired." The man threw back his head and laughed. "I'm not kidding you. I want you to turn over your gun and badge now, and then we'll go in and file the paperwork. I'll call your—"

"What the fucking blue blazes is going on here?" Luke turned to see who the newcomer was and saw Allen coming out of his building. He mouthed the word "chief," and Luke turned to the man.

"I've just relieved your officer of his duties. And then I'm going to take his gun and badge until we can get a replacement for him." Like the officer, the chief laughed too. "You know, it would be nice if one of you would let me in on the big joke. I could certainly use a good laugh about now."

"You're the joke, you dumb shit. You think you can come in here and just fire my men? That's not going to happen. You might want to rethink that bit of stupidity for a minute there. Who the hell do you think would keep the peace? Your kind? I think not." He reached over for Ellis, but Luke put his hand out to stop him. "You might want to think real hard on that one a bit, buddy. I have a gun and the law on my side. You fuck with me and my men and I will make your life a living hell. Might anyway just for you breathing the same air as real people."

Luke felt his temper rise, and his wolf wanted blood. Not just enough to scare the man, but enough to kill. Every time his wolf snarled at him, Luke had to fight really hard to keep him at bay. It wasn't working as well as he needed it to. Trying his best to talk slowly so the idiot would understand how pissed he was, Luke spoke to the cop.

"Let him go or so help me I will rain a terror down on you that will make you hide in a corner and beg for your mommy while you suck your thumb." Luke had spoken softly, but he could see by the look on the cop's face that he'd heard. "Let my brother go. Right. Fucking. Now."

Granger let him go, but he didn't move back. The anger boiling off the man was secondary only to his own. Luke was working extra hard to calm his wolf, but he was having trouble because he wanted to kill the man. Not only had he threatened him and his family, but he'd also made it perfectly clear that he wasn't going to respect his title. When he finally moved back from Ellis, Luke took a step back as well. As both the cop and the chief moved away, the Osborne employee said he'd find him, like that was supposed to scare Luke. That's when Hunter touched his mind.

Are you all right? Luke didn't answer him because he wasn't sure what to say. *Luke, either tell me or I'm coming down there. Slone can feel it too, and she's looking for a gun right now.*

I'm okay. Not fine but okay. There was an altercation and things didn't go well. Still not going well. I'm in trouble here that I might be shot for. But tell Slone that I'm fine and that I'll explain later. Hunter told him he'd try. *Granger, the fucking police chief, just threatened me. Said he was going to make our lives hell. I'm with Ellis now. I don't think he's any happier than I am right now.*

Good. And Granger can try. Luke thought he'd more than try and told Hunter that. *What are you going to do? If he gives you too much trouble you can always have him arrested. I'm sure that there is enough to have the Feds come back and look into him.*

I'm sure there is, but I need a replacement first. The town might be better off without him, but I have no clue. I'm going to have to see about finding someone that wants the job before I go firing him. Hunter didn't answer. *I don't suppose you want the job, do you?*

Fuck no. They both laughed, and after assuring his brother that he was going to be all right and that he'd get back to him later to explain what had happened, they closed the connection. Luke asked Ellis to come with him to his office, and they were both sitting at the conference table when Ellis suddenly looked amused.

"You aren't pissed?" Ellis got up to pace and then went to the small refrigerator that Luke had brought in the day before. As he pulled out a bottle of water and drained it, he stood there for several seconds before he answered.

"I wanted to shift and have his ass for lunch. I have never...Christ. How on earth did you not take him when he said he was going to shoot you?" The bottle hit the rim of the trash can and tipped it over. "I'm going home to go on a run. It's that or...I'll talk to you later."

Nodding, he watched his brother leave his office. Luke got up to see that he made it to his truck all right, then went back to his desk. All the plans he'd had for the day were shot to shit right now. And Luke didn't really care at that point. When Allen came to tell him that the chief had canceled their meeting, Luke was actually disappointed.

~~~

Hank Granger was feeling pretty good about the turn of events. Damned if he didn't want to take out an ad in the local rag about how he'd gotten the better of the fucking mayor. And right there on Main Street too. The guy would learn his place or he'd be run out on a rail. He picked up the phone to call Emmett Osborne.

"Just had a fun-filled morning with your competition. I gotta tell you, there isn't anyone dumber than he seems to be. He even had the balls to threaten me." His partner laughed. "You should have seen him. Nearly pissed himself when I ordered him to back off. I think this one might be as fun as the guy before Conklin. And that mother fucker better keep his mouth shut too."

The story could go any way he wanted it to since nobody would say anything different. It was gospel when he said something, and there wasn't a fool in this town that didn't know that. Hank was the man who got things done, and he would kill you if you didn't agree with him. It was just the way things were done. Conklin, however, was a different story. That guy knew too much and had way too many dirty secrets about everyone.

"I heard all about it from Danny on how he was simply walking by when the Emerson punk jumped him. He said that you tried to arrest that Emerson kid for hitting him. Stupid fuck said he was going to find him in a dark alley one night soon and take his ass out. I'm thinking if he wants that to happen, he'd better lay off the drugs and shit."

Hank had to agree with that. The Gilbert boy had always had a bit too much fun with the recreational drugs. Not to mention, he was skimming Osborne's books too. Hank wondered if Osborne knew that, and decided to bring it up next time he saw the man. Instead, Hank changed the subject from the boy to another pressing matter.

"You still having that meeting with him, the mayor-elect? I canceled mine as soon as I got to my office. I'd hate to have to hurt the little shit, and it'd be all over if I had to sit in a room with him for more than five seconds. You know as well as I do that my temper isn't the best when I'm riled up." Hank did have a moment of unease when he thought of the way the man had practically vibrated with his animal, and the fact that he'd seen more than just a little fur on the bastard. He'd had long canines too, for a second. But Hank figured his gun trumped the guy's big teeth any day of the week.

"I just had Margaret call him. I'm not going to sit in his office all day while he tells me what I have and haven't finished in the way of work. Does he think I got nothing better to do with my time than to run down each and every contract and make sure the work is being done? Fucking little prick. You think he's scared of me?" Hank doubted that but didn't comment on Emmett's wishful thinking. Emmett was an overweight guy who could barely make it from his recliner to the toilet without having to take a rest. "He isn't going to be taking any bids from me anyway. Not so long as you pick the winners for me. Ain't that right? Or did he take that away from you too?"

"No. He's not said a word that I've been privy to. Heard a lot of bullshit, but nothing's been said to me."

Emmett snorted with disgust. "I'm thinking the guy needs to be made gone. We need someone like Conklin back in office. He was a straight shooter."

Conklin, like him, was only out for himself. But Hank agreed that Emerson had to be gotten rid of. The sooner the better too. The cut he got from giving the bids to his friend had put in a nice pool, as well as paid for that wonderful vacation he'd taken his family on last year. And this year he was going to be taking his in-laws as well. There was no way that he could have this much fun on just skimming the books like he did. He needed Emmett as much as Emmett did him.

"You just leave the bids to me. You put in one for that new building the rich cunt wants, right? The one that is supposed to be the library for the school kiddies?"

Emmett told him he had and the amount. "Nice. Nice. I can really use my cut from that. And she doesn't really need a library for them kids anyhow. They already have a really nice one at the school. If she wants to put her name on something, she should come to my office and I can let her put her name on my desk when I have her bent over it fucking her. A bitch like her would be tight too."

They both laughed, knowing that neither of them would get within ten feet of the woman without her husband tearing them a new ass. He was a possessive motherfucker.

They moved on to their plans for the weekend. Fishing and beer. Rarely did their hooks get wet, but they did put away a great deal of beer. And food. Hank had already made arrangements to take up ten of them big subs that Mable put together. Even though she wasn't a human, the woman could put together a nice sammich when she had to. He could almost taste the roast beef one. He'd ordered an extra so he could enjoy it on the drive up.

After about another hour of bullshit, Hank hung up. He had shit to do. First on his list was looking on the interweb to find that necklace his wife wanted for Christmas. His thinking was another man's loss was his gain, and he put in a bid for the thing hoping that nobody was stupid enough to outbid him. Laughing to himself, he decided that he wanted some lunch for himself, and left at a little before noon to go and get it. The thought of Mable's sammich made him want one today, and he headed that way as he took in the lack of activity going on at the construction sites with Osborne's name on them. The man was a card, he'd give him that.

Mable didn't like him. Hell, everybody knew it, but here lately she'd been getting a little lippy with him when he came in. Like her wanting him to pay off his outstanding bill. She was the only person he knew that kept tabs on how much he charged each month. Last time he was in, she told him right off that it was his last freebie. He'd either pay up or no food, and that was final.

He went into the diner and was told to wait a minute. Hank could just about taste his lunch now. When Mabel came out of the back room, he smiled at her as she held his bag.

"It's four hundred and twenty-three dollars." He looked at her, wondering how the hell she'd come to that. "It includes your past bill as well as today. How do you want to pay? I got me a new charge machine and I can take that if you want."

"You know damn good and well I don't carry that much money on me. And I never carry around my credit card while on duty. That kind of shit can get you into trouble. I'll get you next time." He reached for the bag and she pulled it back out of his reach. "Now, Mable, I've had a bad morning so far, and you keeping me from my lunch is not going to go well for you. Just be a good little woman and hand it over nice and easy like."

"You pay or you don't eat. It's as simple as that." He reached for it again and she moved back several steps. If the counter hadn't been between them, he might have gotten it. As it was, he'd have to leap up over it to get her, and his leaping days were well over.

"Give me the fucking food. I'm not in the mood to fuck with you." She turned, went to the large totes that held dirty dishes, and dropped the bag into the top one. "What the fuck? Give that to me this minute or so help me I'll chase you down every time you come out on the streets and give you a ticket for breathing. Hand it over right now or so help me...."

She just stood there. Hank moved to breach her side of the counter when he found himself pinned to the wall. The man holding him didn't look familiar right away. Then he realized it was Pete Skills.

"You'll take your filthy hands off me or I'll shoot you where you stand. Your kind don't touch real people like me." The gun at his side was suddenly torn from his hip, and Pete snarled at him. "You're going to jail for this. You just wait and see if you don't."

Fear made sweat bead on his forehead. His back was starting to get a little damp too, and he tried to ignore the way Pete's eyes seemed to darken. Anger spilled out over him, but it wasn't any competition to the fear he had. Hank finally understood the term "sweating bullets."

"Pay the damned money." Hank had a hard time understanding him, so Pete had to repeat it before he got it. His big teeth seemed to be getting in the way of him talking plainly.

"I don't have to pay shit. She should have to pay me for letting her soil my town." His head banged hard against the wall and he felt his teeth bite into his tongue. "Let me go, you motherfucker, or else."

"Let him go, Pete." The man standing just behind him spoke in a low calming voice, but there was a hardness there that Hank almost envied. "Let the chief go before he pisses his pants."

Pete let him go, but he hit his head against the wall again before he stepped back. Hank turned to the other man to tell him he had it under control when he saw the rich cunt and her husband standing there. She was laughing and Hank wanted to strangle her. But the man seemed to know what he was thinking and stepped in front of her.

"You should keep better track of your animals there, Emerson. One of them might get his ass run over one day." Emerson handed him his holster that was empty. "There was a gun in this when I dropped it. Where the fuck is it?"

"Dropped it? No matter. I'm turning it over to the mayor. I'm pretty sure that when you allow a person to take your gun, you should no longer be able to have it."

Hank tossed the ruined holster on the table and laughed. He hated the way it sounded forced but didn't care at the moment. He turned to Mable, who hadn't said a word since her boyfriend had grabbed him up.

"Where's my lunch?" She glared at him but didn't move to get him anything. "Are you denying me service, Mable? That's not very good business sense to not let your patrons have their food. And you know as well as I do you need me coming in here just for security purposes. A lot can happen when the cops aren't too friendly to you. Might just burn to the ground without us."

She snorted. "Security like yours I can do without. You are as useless as tits on a bore hog, Chief. I told you the last time you were here, you need to pay up. I can't be carrying your ass any longer. When you pay, you can eat. But no more credit. And that means your order for the weekend too. I don't care if you ever set foot in here again. As you can see, I have that under control as well."

"I see how you are. You think that because there's a new alpha in town you're going to show him what you're made of." He lunged at her and she moved back. Hank had a good laugh over that. "Lookee at how brave you are now. You might remember how scared you are right now.

'Cause I got news for you, it ain't nothing to what's gonna happen to you later."

The rich cunt stepped up to him and he glared at her. When she smiled at him, Hank doubled up his fist to teach her a lesson too. She only laughed when he drew back to slam his fist through her head if he had to. He was ready to let it fly when she spoke.

"You'll be dead before you touch me." He felt the chill of her words when she smiled again. Hank watched her as she stared at him and had a feeling that she was right. And the man standing next to her wouldn't have to lift a finger. "You might want to remember how afraid you are right now, Chief, because when I'm finished with you, you'll not have a pot to piss in."

"I'm the law here." She laughed and lunged at him in much the same manner that he had Mable. And just like the older woman, he stepped back as well. She was still laughing as he moved out of the restaurant.

"The whole fucking town is getting a bit too uppity right now. Might have to take them down a peg or two." As he moved to the deli down the street he noticed that a sign in the window had a list on it, and there on the top was his name, just under the heading that said "Deadbeat People," along with the amount he owed. Shit. He had to come up with three hundred bucks for them if he wanted their mediocre sammich, it seemed.

Mother fuck. As he moved home to have his housekeeper make him something to eat, he thought of different ways he was going to get back at each and every one of them. Right at the top of the list was having his men pull each and every one of them over for even having their hair messed up. If they drove. He just realized he'd never seen any of them in a car. Hank decided to look into that right fucking now. Or tomorrow. His belly was telling him that he had to fill it or it would rumble at the worst times.

Chapter 2

Jacklyn Wagner was still working on the project when the janitor came in to empty her trash. He just shook his head and said nothing as she leaned back to let him have the full can. She reached into her desk drawer and pulled out the big bag she'd put there after lunch, and grinned when Max Rogers took it from her. The man was probably the nicest person working there, and she loved spoiling him.

"My wife makes me this perfect meal and I been taking it without a word. Do you know what you're doing to me? I have to tell her what a wonderful sandwich it is and I ain't bit into one of them for over six months. Not to mention you're making me a little fat." He sat down at the little table in her office and opened the bag. "Oh my. Roast beef and Swiss. Jack, you know this is my favorite."

She laughed. "Max, they're all your favorite. And you know that I love you with all my heart. I love the fact that you keep an eye on me. I'm still paying you for saving my ass last year." He waved her off as he took a healthy bite of the sandwich and moaned. "Good, huh?"

"The best. And I didn't do nothing you or about a million other people wouldn't have done. You just happened to be in the wrong place at the wrong time, and I happened to be in the right one. You have to stop spending your hard earned money on me."

Jack thought she had spent her entire life in the wrong place and wrong time but said nothing to Max. She was just grateful that he'd been there for her. And contrary to what he thought, not many people would have come to her rescue.

She'd been going out to her car, the piece of shit that it was, when someone had grabbed her from behind. Jack had been turned so quickly that she'd dropped her bag and her keys. But she fought back. When he'd hit her in the face with something hard she'd seen stars, but she didn't stop fighting him as he ripped her blouse open. The moment she realized she was going to be raped, Max had shouted. The man told him to get the fuck out of there.

"Ain't no business of yours. This is between me and the bitch here." The man slammed her head against her car and told her to shut the fuck up and she might live until he was finished, then tore her clothing off her so that she stood there in only her bra and panties. Then he snapped her arm against the car and she felt it break. Her scream had him cursing and telling her she was going to be dead if she didn't shut the fuck up. She nearly threw up when Max tore him from her before he could make due on his threat. Jack still shivered every time she thought about what she'd seen.

"You okay?" She nodded at him and looked at the drawing in front of her. "You work too hard, you know that, don't you? There is no job worth spending your every waking hour on. I bet they don't even pay you a lot to be here right now. If they pay you at all for working after they close up."

"They don't. And you're right. I'm on my own time on this one. And I have to work this hard if I want to have a place to lay my head at night." Max shook his head and bit into the sandwich again. "Max, can I ask you something?"

"You know you can. But if you're going to ask me again about that night, I'm going to tell you the same as I did before. You hit your head, child. There was no big animal there when that man tried to take what you weren't offering."

Jack nodded, not really believing him. She knew what she'd seen. The big gray wolf had been snapping his teeth at the would-be rapist until he left. And Max was nowhere to be found. Not, at least, until the police had arrived. She had wondered for weeks after if she'd really hit her head that hard, or had the man sitting before her all prim and proper like shifted into a big wolf.

She'd gotten fifty-three stitches and had had to wear a sling on her arm for a month from the broken wrist. Her boss had not been happy about her being on pain meds, so she'd had to suffer through it after the first day or so in order to keep her job. She looked down at the scar on her arm that was a constant reminder of how not to be a victim. Max asked her what she had wanted.

"I was wondering if you'd heard from your son lately. You said he was getting a new boss. I was wondering how that was working for him." It wasn't what she was going to ask him and she was pretty sure he knew it. As he told her about the new boss and his wife, she sort of zoned out until he mentioned Sommersville.

"My brother lives there." He looked surprised. "He moved there right after Mom died. I think it was to get away from Dad, but he said things are starting to look good in the town. He has a new boss too. I have no idea what he does, however. I've not spoken to him in a good long time."

"What's his name? Maybe Dan knows him." She smiled and told him Allen Wagner. "Well, hell yeah he knows him. Did you know that your brother works for the mayor? He's a good boy, your brother. I met him the last time I was there visiting. I'll have to tell him I know you the next time I go there."

She nodded, and a few minutes later Max moved on with his cart. Jack sat staring at the campaign she'd been assigned and wondered how the hell she was supposed to make this work. How did one make adult diapers sexy? When nothing came to mind, she thought of her brother.

Allen was younger than her by only seventeen months. They'd been the best of friends when they were smaller. Then when their mom had gotten sick, he'd turned into this jerk. She supposed it had something to do with the fact that her mom had always spoiled Allen. He'd been her little boy, and she had simply been Jack. And the nonsense of little girls being loved by their daddies had never been true about her and her father. He'd been a bastard when she was little, and hadn't changed much when she'd gotten older. But Allen had…Allen had been Allen. He'd turned to alcohol first, then drugs. By the time she'd left home, he'd been arrested more times than she'd been out, and she'd had enough.

Right after she'd been called home seven years ago to "deal with him," she found out that their mom was sick. Cancer had taken its toll on her and she'd never said a word to anyone. By the time Jack had found out, it was much too late for the former beauty queen, and she died as quietly as she'd lived as Allen Wagner Senior's wife. And Allen, the son, had taken it very badly.

She supposed it had not helped matters when she'd left him in jail the last time he'd called her for bail money. Jack had bailed him out so many times that she was sick of doing it. Dad had told her she should have more compassion for Allen, as he'd lost his mom, but when she explained to him it was her mom too, he'd slapped her and told her not to be disrespectful of the dead. That was the last straw, and she'd left them both to deal on their own.

Then about four years ago she'd gotten a post card from Allen telling her where he was living, and asking if she'd come to see him. The post cards kept coming…she'd read them, of course, but she never responded to them. She wasn't going to be pulled back into that life. Not now, not ever again.

Jack reached into her bottom drawer and pulled out the small shoe box. Inside it was every one of the cards he'd sent her over the years in the order that she'd received them, including the first one that she'd had to dig out of the trash. She took the last one she'd gotten two days ago and read it again.

I'm doing well and have a new boss. He's really nice and seems to be trustworthy. I've yet to tell him about my arrest a few years back. I'm just hoping he will not fire me. Christmas is in a few weeks and I'm hoping you'll make your way to come out to see me. I miss you. Allen.

There were times when she missed him as well. Putting the card back into the little box, she closed it and got back to work. Thinking over what might have been was not going to keep her in a job.

It was nearly five in the morning when she had done all she could with the advertisement. She wasn't happy with it and doubted that her boss would be either. Why he'd take on such a small client was beyond her, and especially one that was going to get sued soon when someone saw the packaging he was using. The thing looked just like the national brand all the way down to the color of it. Jack was even sure the name was stretching it a bit. The only difference was the s on the end had an apostrophe.

As she rushed home to get a change of clothes, she thought of all the things she had to do this weekend...laundry, dusting, and catching up on some much needed sleep. But as she neared her apartment she began to worry. There were a great many cops on her street, as well as a lot of her neighbors standing outside of their homes in their robes and slippers. Plus there were news crews everywhere. And then she saw the smoke.

Parking her car in the middle of the street, she got out and rushed to the building. She had to see if she could save something. Everything she had, everything she'd ever owned, was in that burning building.

No one tried to stop her as she moved into the smoking inferno, and she had started up to the third flight of stairs when she nearly fell over the body of one of the firemen on the stairs. He was lying there unconscious, with blood on his shirt. Jack looked up the stairs where her things were and back at the man. She shook her head, grabbed him by the shoulders, and pulled him down the stairs as best she could. The man had to weigh a ton, she thought. But she pulled and pulled until she got him to the bottom set of stairs.

Her body was hurting by the time she got to the last landing. She tried her best to cover her face from the smoke, but it was getting the better of her. As she started down the last few steps to fresh air, she started to feel dizzy. Sitting down, she tried to think how to get out without leaving him behind. Then there was a shadowy figure coming up the stairs.

"I think he fell." The big fireman had on a mask and goggles so she couldn't see his face, but he nodded and asked her something, which she could hardly hear over the roaring in her head. When she asked him to repeat himself, she felt herself being lifted up and thrown over his massive shoulder. The fireman that she'd been pulling was left behind. Jack started to struggle against the man holding her.

"You have to go back and get him." He said something else, and Jack kicked him. He dropped her and she sat there stunned for several seconds as the air came back into her lungs. It didn't help. It was hot and painful. Her lungs felt on fire from it and all the smoke. The fireman reached for her again, and she crawled to the fallen man.

"You can pull me and I'll hold onto him. I'm not going to leave him here to burn up." He said something else, and she grabbed the fireman that she'd named Carl. "You just help me drag him out and then I'll go with you."

He finally took the man by the shoulders and lifted him up. When he had him over his shoulder as he'd been carrying her, she held onto his belt when he pointed to it. Jack had to try three times before she could get it into her hand. The thought of just simply lying down was making her sick. When the fireman turned to take them to safety, Jack held on as best she could, but lost her grip and fell. It was the last thing she remembered as her head hit something hard.

~~~

Allen was on hold with the police station. He hated the chief of police more than he did anyone. But the mayor needed some answers, and Allen said he'd get them for him. And if Luke wanted it, he'd damn well get it.

The other line was ringing and Allen was almost afraid to put this one on hold to take it. But when it was answered he turned to look at the door behind him. Luke Emerson was one of the best bosses he'd ever had. Not only did he treat him like a person, but he also listened to his opinions, something no one had ever done before. When the woman he'd been talking to came back on the line, she told him that Chief Granger was too busy to come to the phone, and that he should perhaps call in the morning. He was ready to tell her that this was the fourth time he'd called when Luke came out of his office. He looked…Allen hung up on the woman.

"There's been an accident." Allen stood up then sat down. "Do you have a sister named Jacklyn Wagner?"

"Yes. I call her Jack, but that's her name. Jacklyn Maggie Wagner. She never liked her first name after Dad told her he named her for a dog he'd had as a kid. She said that if anyone called her that again, she'd make the dog look like a kitten." Allen shut his mouth, just realizing that he was babbling. "Is she…is she dead?"

"No. But she's hurt badly. They've got her in the burn unit at Mercy General in her town. Her apartment building was on fire and they found her in the hall with one of the firefighters. She was apparently trying to rescue him."

"That would be my sister. She would leap where no others would when she thought someone needed her. She did for me enough. Up until I fucked up so badly that she washed her hands of me. Not that I blame her, but I wished she'd just talk to me." He closed his mouth again and Luke sat on the edge of his desk. Allen felt as if someone had put a vise on his chest and he couldn't breathe right.

"They have you as next of kin, and they were asking for you to come to see her. They think the sooner you get there, the better."

Allen stood up and got his coat. He was just going to the door when he heard Luke say his name. Allen felt the last five years of his life come crashing down on him.

"I have no idea what to do. I can't help her. I can't even get to her. I can't drive. I don't have a car. I could go on my bike, but I don't know how I'd get her back here. I suppose she could ride on the handle bars like she used to ride me when we were kids, but that might not work now that she's bigger. But she hates me. She won't even return my cards I send her. I think I really fucked up with her. I know I did. She should hate me for all the shit I did to her. I don't—" He felt his teeth rattle as Luke shook him.

"Get a grip." Allen nodded and was pushed into a chair. "Okay. You can't drive but I can. And I'm not sure what happened between the two of you, but she must have felt something for you if she had them call you."

Allen nodded. He had no idea why anyone would call him when they needed help. He could barely hold himself up most of the time. But Luke was in charge now and he'd see to things for him. Not that he wanted to depend on anyone again, but this was his sister, his only sister, and she needed him.

"I can give you the directions to her place. I used to go there a long time ago, but not in a long while. I wanted to, but without a license I don't do much traveling." He reached for a piece of paper to write the address on when Luke said his name again.

"You're going too. I'm not going to go to the hospital and bring back a strange woman. A strange and hurt woman. She would more than likely not come with me, and they said you were going to have to be there. You're her brother. You can do this." Allen nodded. "Is there anyone else you should be calling? Your mom? Dad?"

"My mom died when I was a teenager. My dad? He hated Jack more than he did me most of the time." Allen had resolved himself to the fact that he'd done this all to himself, but his dad had been a prick. He decided that if he had to he'd call him, but not before. "I'm...when do you think we should leave?"

"Now if you're ready. I've already contacted my brother and he's going to keep an eye on things while we're gone. Slone said that if you need the plane, just call and she'll have it ready to bring her back. I told her that we'd see when we got there."

"You mean if she lives." Luke hesitated and Allen felt his heart twist. "How bad is she hurt? I need to know. I don't want to know, but I need to know."

"Her lungs are badly burned and she hit her head on something and fell onto a burning piece of timber. The doctor said she'd be all right if she could make it for the next twenty-four hours, but he wasn't sure. She's in intensive care now. There was a great deal of damage done to her lungs, as I've said, and they have her on a breather to help her."

"And the man she tried to save? Did he make it?" Luke nodded. "Good. If she makes it that will make her feel like this was worth it. Like I said, my sister is the best there is."

They left within the hour. Luke dropped him off at his house and said he'd be back to get him. Allen was shoving things into his suitcase when his phone rang. He answered without checking the caller ID. His nerves were shot.

"You gonna tell me that your sister was hurt or was you hoping that I'd just see it on the news like I did?" Allen closed his eyes and sat on the bed. "I don't like the fact that you shut me out of your lives. I'm your father no matter how much I can't stand either of you. I have a right to know when she's been hurt. Same as I would expect her to tell me if you're dead of an overdose or something."

"I didn't tell you because I didn't know if you'd care." Allen looked at the clothes he was putting in the case and took out the pair of pants and folded them. He decided right then and there that he wasn't going to take his dad's shit any longer. He was twenty-four years old. "Why are you really calling? You can't care a shit if she's dead or alive."

"I don't like that language coming from my kids." Allen snorted, a nice little habit he'd picked up from Luke. "You think this is funny, boy? You aren't too big for me to beat, you know."

"What I know is that you try it, old man, and it will be the last thing you do." His dad sputtered, and Allen heard the doorbell peal. He stood up and moved toward it as he finished with his dad. "Don't call me again. If you do, I'll have my number changed and you'll have no one."

Allen closed his phone and put it into his pocket as he answered the door. Telling Luke that he'd be just a few more minutes, he put the last of the things he thought he'd need into the case and zipped it closed. He had no idea how long he'd be there, but however long he had, he was going to try and talk to his sister. He knew as surely as he was standing there that someone had called him by mistake.

The ride wasn't that long, but long enough for Allen to think of all the stuff he'd done to Jack. First and foremost he'd been a real ass to her when Mom had died. But he'd been so lost without her that he'd taken it out on Jack. Their mom had been the buffer between him and his dad, and when she was gone, Allen Senior had taken his meanness out on him. It was bad enough that he'd done nothing to save his mother, much less his sister, but he'd really failed them both the moment he'd taken drugs into his system.

"What does she do?" Allen looked at Luke when he spoke. "Your sister. What does she do for a living?"

"Graphic design. She works for an advertising firm and she designs ad campaigns. She can draw about anything. I never really understood why she'd gone into advertising as a marketing associate, but I guess it paid the bills." Luke nodded. "I haven't seen my sister in years. Almost five now. I wasn't a great kid, and I wasn't nice to her at all. If someone called me, it had to be mistake. It's doubtful that she would have put my name on her list to be notified. I deserve whatever she feels for me."

"You said she never answered your letters. How many did you send her?" Allen felt stupid that he'd said those things to Luke, but now that it was out there, he would tell him.

"Right after I got out of the clinic to dry out, I started to write her daily. I never sent those, of course, but I did write her. Then when I'd moved here, I started sending her post cards once a week. Most of the time it would just be that I was fine and what I'd done that day. Then as the years went by, I just sent them monthly. The last one, I invited her to come see me for Christmas."

"She doesn't sound like a very nice person." Allen shook his head. "She could have answered you at least once, if only to tell you to stop writing her."

"For that reason alone I kept writing her. She never told me to stop, so I didn't." Allen watched the trees fly by them. "She was good to me. All my childhood she was good to me. And a few times she took the brunt of Dad's temper for something I did. I never appreciated her at all. Not ever. I was cruel to her most of the time, and the only time I had anything to do with her was to bail me out of one jam or another. The last time...she left me in jail the last time I saw her. It was probably all that saved my life. No, that's not right. It did save my life."

Luke didn't say anything for a while, and Allen thought of the man he'd been celled with. Allen had been just eighteen then and his cellmate, a tall, built man, had eyed him for an hour before he stood up and slammed him back against the wall. He held him a foot above the floor until Allen no longer had the strength to struggle. Then he let him go by dropping him on the floor.

"You want me to fuck you in the ass?" Allen had crawled away from him, sobbing. "You think you can stop me if I want to? I've a good mind to show you just what can happen to idiots like you."

As he started to unbuckle his pants, Allen tried to get someone to come for him to save him. The man just laughed. When he didn't move again, Allen looked up at him when his belt hit him in the face. The pain caused stars to dance in his vision, but he never turned from the man. He was terrified to think what he might have done to him at that moment.

"You wanna kill yourself, do it here instead of the prison where you're headed. That way somebody will be able to claim your slimy ass. Otherwise, it might be months before anybody gives a shit that you're dead." Allen watched him walk back to the bed and sit down. "The rate you're going, you'll be butt fucked before the first night. Then some queer will give you something that will either kill you or make you wish you were dead. Provided you don't hang yourself first. You will though. Hang yourself, I mean. A shit weed like you wouldn't stand a night behind bars."

"I could do it." The man laughed. "You think I'm not tough enough? I got news for you, I'm plenty tough enough."

The man stood up and pulled out his dick. Allen had pissed his pants. The man never raped him, but he did talk to him. All night. And when he was let go the next morning, a mistake that Allen had forever been grateful for, he walked out with a new outlook on life. It was the last time he'd ever been behind bars and the last time he'd ever taken any kind of drug or alcohol into his body. But he'd fucked up his relationship with the one person in the world who had ever meant more to him than his parents did. Jack had been and always would be his hero.

Chapter 3

Luke sat in the hall while he waited on Allen. He'd gone in to see his sister about five minutes ago and had not returned yet. The doctor had told him that she could only have a visitor once an hour and only for five minutes. Plus, in order to see her, Allen had had to dress from head to toe in sterile gear. It was a precaution, the doctor had said, as her burns were not that bad. But they didn't want her to catch anything. Her body was having a hard enough time simply functioning on its own, which anyone could see it wasn't doing. Allen told him there were enough machines hooked to her that he was sure it was all that was keeping her alive. Luke had held onto Allen as the doctor had told him what his sister had been dealing with since they'd brought her in.

"She's got some burns on her cheek and one on her shoulder, but those will heal with minimal scarring. Her lungs are what have us worried. She took in a great deal of smoke trying to save that firefighter." Luke watched Allen as the doctor explained. "She will have to have treatments for the rest of her life because of the damage, but she will be able to function well enough, so long as she's careful that she doesn't get a bad cold or anything. But right now…I'm sorry, son, but right now her chances of recovering are very slim. She's in a bad way, and though she might recover, I give her only about a three-percent chance."

Luke stood up when his legs started to cramp up. He was hungry too. Moving down the hall in the direction that Allen had gone he saw the nurse's station, but it was empty of anyone. Turning, Luke looked into the glassed in area. He recognized Allen right away. The man sat straighter than his Aunt Mary did at Sunday dinner. But it was the woman in the bed that took his breath away. She was, quite simply, beautiful.

Even with the bandages on her head, he could see that she had dark hair like Allen's. Her nose, what he could see of it, was small and button-like. He moved closer to the glass, and was startled when a nurse asked him if she could help.

"I'm here with Allen Wagner. That's his sister." She asked him if he wanted to go in as well and he was nodding before he thought better of it. He was dressed and moving into the room before too many minutes passed, and he stood near Allen.

"The doctor said I should talk to her. I don't know what to say, so I've been telling her about my week with you." Allen sounded as if he'd been crying. "She's going to be all right, isn't she?"

Luke nodded, mesmerized by her. When he moved closer to the bed, he nearly backed away again when he caught her scent. He looked at Allen to see if he could smell it too. But, of course, the man was holding his sister's hand and barely paying any attention to him.

Christ, she was his mate. Luke reached for his dad, not sure what else to do.

I just found her. His dad asked him who. *My mate. She's...she might die and I just found her. I don't know what do to.*

Can you convert her? He told him where she was and what had happened. *She'll be all right, son. And once you convert her over to being your mate, that lung problem will go away. You want me to come up there with you? I can be there soon. Just keep an eye on her and I'll be there soon.*

No, I...Christ, Dad. She's beautiful. His dad took offense to that and told him of course she was. *No, I mean...Dad, you should see her. Even hurt the way she is, she's simply the most beautiful creature I've ever seen. I can't see her eyes, but I'm betting that they're dark like mine. Her hair is almost a blue black. Her wolf would be gorgeous. I know that looks aren't everything, but she is perfect.*

You have to claim her before you can go running naked with her, you know that right? Luke flushed and told him he knew that. *I'm coming up. I won't tell Hunter or the others, but I gotta see her now. I can...where the hell are you, anyway?*

Luke told him and about how long it took to get there. It never occurred to him to tell him not to come. Once his dad decided on a course of action, there was no stopping him. And Luke decided that he wanted his dad there with him more than anything. He was glad that he'd told him he wasn't telling Hunter. If she didn't make it, he wasn't sure he could stand to have them around him right then.

"Can you save her?" Luke looked over at Allen, who was staring at his sister. "I know what you are. I mean, I think I know what you are. You can't live in our town and not hear things. Are you?"

"Am I what?" Allen looked at him, and Luke felt as if he were staring at his very soul. Neither of them blinked, and when Allen finally looked away, Luke felt as if he'd been released from a tight hug. "You want to know an answer to something, then ask me. I'm not going to assume anything right now."

"There are rumors that you and your family came here to be in charge of the other wolves in town. I've never…I don't think I have met any of them but…I guess Pete was in charge before you, then before him, I don't know. But you know how things are. And Conklin hated them, all of them." Luke told him that Conklin was a fool. "Yeah, I got that on my own. But I didn't want to be misinformed. So I tried to find something, anything on you when you hired me. There isn't a lot out there. Less if you take out the women's books."

Luke looked at Jack before saying anything. "She's my mate. Do you know what that is? I mean, have you found much on that?"

"Just things that were referred to in those books. I don't normally go for all that bodice ripping stuff, but it was all I could find. She's your other half, right?" Luke nodded. "Other than that, I'm clueless. But if you can save her, then I'd very much like for you to do it."

"I'm a werewolf." Allen didn't look at him but nodded. "I need you to understand, so I'd very much like it if you looked at me." Allen didn't look, but he did speak.

"I'm…I don't want her to die. I know that she more than likely hates me and I can't find a single reason why she shouldn't, but I love her with all my heart." He looked then, and Luke could see the anguish on his face. "You're going to have to change her into what you are. I get that. She's going to have to be hurt more in order for that to work as well. That too I understand. Right now the thought of you doing whatever it is you're going to do scares the shit out of me, but I think it's her only hope.

And if what I've read is true, you can't help but want to make her better. And she will be, right? If you change her?"

"Yes. But you also have to understand that it may quicken her death too." Allen brushed at the tears as he nodded. "Allen, she'll be a werewolf like I am. If she's mad at you, she could kill you without any problems. She'll be my mate. I'm not going to be able to take that back, no matter what you may think right now."

"You can save her by changing her. Jack might be really pissed at me for this, and if she never talks to me again, I don't care so long as she will live." Allen stood up just as the nurse came into the room. He looked at him. Luke nodded, and Allen looked so relieved that he wanted to guide him to a chair.

Luke looked at the nurse. "We're going to transport her closer to home. Mr. Wagner would very much like for you to make the arrangements, and I'll have the doctor whose care she'll be under give you a call."

She stared at him for several seconds before she nodded and left them. Allen started laughing, and Luke looked at him with a quirked brow. He was still laughing when he finally answered.

"You used that mind thing on her, didn't you?" Luke said nothing as Allen laughed harder. "Yeah, you did, and I love it. It's all the books can talk about. How this guy made them do this or some crap like that. Compulsion, I think it's called. Have you ever used that thing on me?"

"It is, and no I have not. And in the future, it's not funny when I make others do what I want them to do. You should have respect for my awesomeness." That, of course, made him laugh harder, and Luke joined him this time. They both sobered quickly when the doctor came to the window and knocked. Luke had a feeling it was going to be more difficult to convince this man than it had been the nurse.

~~~

Hunter wasn't just worried for the woman. She was in bad shape and might not make it at all during this conversion, but he worried for his brother. Luke was already looking like a man who had lost it all. And he knew that he'd not slept well either. Hunter tried to get him to stand back when the gurney was loaded onto the plane.

"I have to be with her." Hunter nodded but pulled him back anyway. "Please, I don't want to have to hurt you, but I will, damn it, if you don't fucking leave me alone."

"You're in their way." Luke looked at the three men and then back at him. "Come with me, and when they have her loaded, you can go in. But for now, you're slowing them down when they're only trying to work. The longer this takes because you're in their way, the longer it will be before you can be with her. Come on, Luke."

Luke nodded and let him pull him back further. He held onto his brother just a little longer after the men came out of the plane too. The need to comfort him was overwhelming. The others, all of them, seemed to feel the same way and came to give him physical support as well.

"I don't know if I can do this." Hunter had a feeling he was thinking about changing the woman and just having her as a mate. "I've never even bitten a woman before during sex. I mean, I know it's in our nature but…Christ, I'm going to kill her."

"No, you're not. You're going to shift as soon as the plane is in the air, then you're going to convert her. We're all here for you. And Dan said that he'd be there as soon as we land." Hunter was so glad that Slone had thought of bringing Dan with them to drive Luke's truck back. It would have been a real bitch to have had to come back and get it, especially if she didn't make it.

As soon as the pilot said they were ready, they all got into the seats. When the lights went off, indicating that they were up high enough, Luke stood up.

"I'm going to be there with you." Luke nodded at his dad. "And so will Hunter. I don't think you'll need us, but you might want someone there to steady you when you're done."

"I want to be there too." Hunter had forgotten about Allen and started to tell him no. But Luke nodded. Hunter didn't think it was a good idea. But it was the man's sister and everything they were doing was because he'd allowed it.

"I'm going to warn you now, Allen. She's going to scream. She might even beg to be let die. But her screaming is going to hurt you. Hurt all of us." Allen paled when Luke spoke to him. "But we do this or she will die. I'm going to have to hurt her in ways that will make the change happen, and she's going to hurt more than she does now. I'm not trying to scare you, but I do want you to know what you're going to see and hear."

"I want to...I need to be with her. I need to know that...I just need to be with her." Luke nodded. "I want to be there for you as well. When this is all finished, we'll be related, you and I."

"You can't stop him once it begins, son." Hunter looked at his dad when he cleared his throat to speak.

With a short nod from him, his dad continued. "He's going to bite her in the leg first, then her belly. That's what's going to have her screaming. And if you try to stop him, or even beg him to stop, you're going to sign your sister's death warrant as surely as if you pulled out a gun and shot her. I'm not kidding you when I say that this is not pretty, like a vamp would do. A bite to the neck a few times then poof, a lady vamp; but this…we're tough, we make tough mates."

"I understand." Hunter hoped to Christ he did, because he would take the man down if he tried to stop this. Luke would more than likely kill him too if he tried. His wolf would be very unstable when this began. And being on a plane at ten thousand feet was not an ideal place to make a conversion.

They moved to the back of the plane where the bed was, and Luke went into the bathroom. When he came out a few minutes later, he was his wolf.

"We've nearly put the bed on the floor for you so it would be easier. Get on up there with her, but be careful of your paws. There isn't any reason you should crush her any while this other is going on." Luke leapt up on the bed and stood over her. He kept staring at her, and his dad moved up behind him. When he lifted her leg up for him to take, Luke whimpered. "I know, son, this is about the hardest thing you'll ever do other than waiting for your first child to be born. But like the rest of us, you can hear her heart slowing. This was just too much on her. Either do it or we stop before it's too late for you both."

Luke lunged forward and took her leg into his mouth. Jack screamed. Not a loud scream, as her voice was raw from the smoke, but enough to make Luke and the rest of them hurt for her. When his dad said to move back after a few minutes, they exposed her belly. Before Luke could go there, Allen stepped up and hugged Luke. Then he left the room. Hunter sent Jarrett out to keep him under control if need be.

As soon as Luke bit into her flesh, she came up off the bed, screaming. This time it echoed around the small cabin over and over until she finally fell back on the bed. Luke never let her go the entire time, and Hunter knew what it was costing him. He didn't have any doubt that if he had to hurt Slone like this, he'd rather kill himself. His respect for his brother went up exponentially.

She's not going to make it. He looked over at Slone when she spoke to him through their connection. *I can hear her heart. She's barely hanging on. Oh, Hunter, what will he do? He can't love her as yet, but she's his mate. I don't think I could do this to you if I had to.*

I was thinking the same thing about you. I just…I love you very much, Slone. With all my heart. And I don't know what he'll do. This will devastate him. He pulled her into his arms as they watched. *I really have no idea how he's hanging on to her like this. He has never spoken a word to her, never touched her before this, and here he is, on the verge of losing it all.*

"Luke, let her go. It was too much on her." Hunter felt the tears stream down his face when his dad approached the bed. "Come on, son; you tried and she was just too weak. You did all you could for her."

The low growl made Hunter's own wolf stir. He was protecting his sire, and Hunter had to work hard to calm him. But when Luke jerked his mouth in her belly and growled again, Jack moaned. His dad moved up closer but never touched either of them. When he cocked his head toward her, he turned to Hunter and smiled.

"Well, I'll be damned." Hunter started to ask his dad what when he heard it too. Her heart beat was picking up.

Not only that, but he could see the burns on her face starting to heal as well. She was going to make it. Christ good Lord, she was going to make it.

After another ten minutes Luke let her go. He never left her side but lay on the bed over her while she continued to improve. Five minutes before the plane was to land, Hunter went to get Allen. She was far enough along now that anyone could see that she was going to wake up and be just fine.

As soon as he opened the door, Allen stood up. He looked like he'd been preparing for the worst. But when he nodded and invited him in the room, Allen sat back down. Hunter sat down beside him. The man had been through just as much as they had, and he was only a human.

"She's going to be pissed." Hunter didn't know the woman, but he was pretty sure her brother was right. She had to have a strong will to have survived what she'd been through in the last few days. "I don't know what to tell her about this, but I'm taking full responsibility. And Jack always did have a temper that would peel paint off the wall. Now that she's a wolf...." Allen shivered, and Hunter laughed.

"You saved her life." Allen shook his head. "Yes, you did. Had you not given Luke permission, he would have had to wait to speak to me before he could convert her. Without permission, he could have been killed by the pack for doing what he did. It's the law of our kind. You do not convert someone on a whim, nor do you do it without permission. You saved them both by telling him to do it."

"Would you have been all right with him changing her?" Hunter nodded, but told him he'd have had to get permission from the were council as well. "That would have been too late, wouldn't it? While—what I'm assuming is as much a governing thing like what I work for is—while we waited for them to answer, she would have died."

"More than likely, yes. They can take their time on things like this because they need to be sure they're doing the right thing. In this case it was the only thing, but it would still have taken too long." Allen sat there for several more seconds until the seatbelt light came on. He buckled in when the rest of them did, and no one mentioned Luke. He wouldn't leave her until he had to and even then, Hunter doubted he'd do it willingly.

As soon as they had Jack in their home, someone went to the pack house to gather some clothing for Luke. He couldn't have taken her to his room at the pack house, and Hunter and Slone could help him take care of her. She was going to live, but Jack was a long way from recovered. As Luke settled in the chair next to Jack's bed, Hunter and Slone moved down to their living room and left the young couple alone.

"She is really strong." Hunter nodded as he pulled Slone into his lap. "I remember the first time I woke up. I was in the hospital still, but I could swear I could smell every meal they'd served in that room for a year."

"Me too. I mean I was born a wolf, but after your first shift, things seem to get more everything. Brighter, louder, and even more intense. Dad had to lock me in my room for the first night. I wanted to go out and kill every bug outside." Slone laughed, and he put his hand over her still flat belly. "I love you."

"And I'm sort of fond of you too." Slone snuggled in his arms. "I'm going to help her. She might not care for me at first, I'm betting, but I'm going to help her. She's the closest thing to a sister I've ever had."

"She'll love you. What's not to love?" She snorted. "I love you, so she'll have to. And while we're talking about her, I wanted to tell you how much I like her brother too. He could have made it hell on Luke, yet he supported him all the way."

"They didn't get along, Jack and Allen. I think it has to do with the dad, but I'm not sure." Hunter had heard Allen talking on the phone with someone just before they'd gotten on the plane, and it was heated to say the least. "We might want to have him come here to stay for a while too. I'm not sure, but I think it would be safer for him."

Hunter thought so too and was glad Slone had thought of it. "Luke said he was having some issues with the chief and Emmett Osborne, of Osborne Construction. I think for the time being I'll keep someone on them as well. I don't want anyone to get into trouble right now."

Hunter went to the office and made a few calls. He also had Pete come over when he could. The older man had been there most of his life, and could more than likely tell him of every skeleton in every closet in this town. He said he'd come by for dinner. Just as Hunter hung up, his dad came into the room.

"You think this girl will be like your mate?" Hunter wasn't sure what he was asking and asked him to clarify. "You know, friendly like Slone. Open to having me around? I know you said I could stay here for my life, but there was just the two of you before. Now there's another couple here."

"You think she won't like you?" That surprised him because Hunter knew that everyone liked his dad. "I think she'll love you a great deal. Just like Slone does. But I doubt this is a permanent thing. Luke will want his own home with her. But I don't think they'd be a problem anyway. Why do you ask?"

"She has a daddy."

Hunter started to tell him that was a stupid reason to think someone wouldn't like him when it dawned on him. "You think because her and her dad aren't close she won't be with you." His dad shrugged. "Dad, I think she's going to welcome you into her life in much the same way Slone did. Her relationship with her dad is not going to have any bearing on you and her at all, other than she hates him and not you. Allen likes you."

"Yeah, and I like the kid too. But Allen said their dad is a real bastard. I'd adopt that boy too if he'd let me. Never have seen a brother do so much without being sure of her love for him." Hunter had thought of that too. Allen had done a great deal for his sister, and it would more than likely not strengthen their relationship very much at the beginning. He felt sorry for the kid and hoped that he'd be okay.

"I think she's going to be just fine. She's going to need some adjustment time, I guess, but she should fit right in with the rest of us. And of all the men in this family, Luke is the most patient of us all. He'll bring her around."

"I hope so. But I have a feeling that she's going to be harder to tame than one of them wild wolves out there in the yard, and a good deal less receptive of Luke. He might have to be a little more...I was going to say firm with her, but I'm thinking he might have to beat her butt a few times to get her attention."

Hunter stared at his dad. He wanted Luke to beat his mate's butt? That just didn't sound like him at all. But when he stood up and moved out of the room, Hunter called him back. His dad turned and asked him what he wanted.

"You don't mean that. You don't think that Luke will have to beat his mate to get her to understand...I don't know what she'd have to understand, but I doubt beating her ass will do it." His dad shrugged. "Dad?"

"I didn't say it had to be painful, I just said he had to get her attention. Nothing like a naked bottom on your knees to make a man want to have a woman see reason more than anything." Hunter flushed and thought of Slone over his knees, and his dad laughed. "See? You're already thinking about ways to get that little miss of yours to listen to you, aren't you?"

"I don't think we're talking about the same thing." His dad laughed harder and left the room. A few minutes later, Slone came in and she smiled at him.

"Your dad said you needed me for something." Hunter laughed. "He said it was important. Is it?"

"It is. Come here, wife. I have a desire to bend you over my knee and see how pink I can make that pretty ass of yours." She stood there for several seconds before she turned back to the door. He thought for sure she was going to leave him when he heard the lock click in place.

"We need to go over this very thoroughly, I think." He nodded and moved back from the desk. "And when you're done with my bottom, my nipples could use a little help too. Do you think you could, I don't know, suckle them until they're nice and pink too? If we're going to do some research on this, we should be very detailed."

When she was within touching distance, he pulled her over his knees. As soon as he had her there, he swatted her ass hard. She squealed but didn't move off. He smacked her again.

"Stand up and strip for me." She did as he said, and when she bent at the waist and pulled her pants and panties off, he could see where his hand had connected with her. Christ, his cock felt full enough to explode. Pulling her back to him, he turned her and suckled at her naked breasts as she curled her fingers into his hair. He looked up at her when she jerked him back.

"I'm going to come like this if you keep this up. Wouldn't you like it better if we were in our nice big bed and you were eating my pussy?" He nodded. "Or you could just take me here."

Slone sat on his desk and opened her legs for him. Hunter moved his chair closer and buried his mouth over her. When she cried out, he knew that he'd be deep inside of her before long.

"Slone, have I told you lately that I love you?"

She grinned. "Shut up, love, and do me. I've a powerful need to bring the house down around your ears." There was no way he was going to let her go around with that sort of need, and he took her clit into his mouth and bit her. She came, crying out his name.

Hunter decided right then and there that his dad was right. He wasn't going to tell him of course. His head was big enough. But he'd been right about this.

Chapter 4

Jack felt her body come back to her in small increments. First she felt her fingers, then her hands. By the time she'd made her way to her head, she was turning it to look at what could be weighing her down so much. The top of a head startled her. Then the small laugh to her right had her turning that way. Her eyes seemed to have something wrong with them, because everything seemed to be too…everything.

"Allen?" He nodded but only stared at her. "What are you doing in my room, and who the hell is this?"

The man—because she suddenly had no doubt it was a man—moved. When he stretched out his body over hers, Jack moaned. There was no help for it, she told herself, and she'd been without sex for….

"Where am I? I know this isn't my house…it burned down." Allen nodded again. "Do you think you could do something more than act like a fucking bobble head right now? I swear to Christ, I am about two seconds from freaking the fuck out."

"What's the last thing you remember?" Jack looked at the man again when he spoke. She thought maybe she was dead, because there was no way in hell a man like this one would end up in her bed. When he laughed, she had a very real feeling he could read her mind. "Jacklyn, what's the last thing you remember?"

"It's Jack, and I remember everything. Except how I ended up in this bed with my brother sitting there staring at me like I have three heads."

Allen finally spoke and she asked him what he'd said.

"I said, I'm just thrilled to death that you're not dead. You've no idea how close...Christ, Jack, you went into a burning building. What the hell did you think was going to happen?"

"This from a man who continued to do drugs after several of his friends were killed by them. Drove a car stoned when he had just totaled his car the week before." She felt horrible by what she said the moment he stood up. "Allen, I'm—"

"I'm sure you can handle this from here on out. Right, Luke?" Allen didn't wait for an answer but left her. She turned to the man, who she was assuming was Luke, when he sat up. Christ holy shit. He didn't have a shirt on.

"You should know that he's been sitting in that chair for the last five days just waiting for you to wake up. Never left, only to go to the bathroom. He had his meals brought in here so he'd be close if you needed him." Luke stood up and stretched again. Jack watched him as every muscle on his body seemed to move with it. When he caught her looking at him, he grinned again. "I could join you in that bed if you'd like. Nothing right now sounds better than to taste every part of you."

"No." When she realized how loud she'd been, she cleared her throat and tried again. "No. That won't be necessary. If you could just tell me how I can get home...well, that's not going to work. I couldn't get there even if I had a ride to do it in. And I'm pretty sure my car has been impounded. I sort of left it in the middle of the road. And I'm babbling. If you don't mind, I'd like to leave now please. I'm not really sure why I'm here but…why am I here?"

"I brought you here. It was easier for me to take care of you here rather than in a hospital. You never answered me. What's the last thing you remember?" She closed her eyes, suddenly exhausted. He asked her if she was all right.

"Just peachy. The last thing I remember…my apartment was covered in smoke and there were firefighters everywhere. I don't know…I got inside because I wanted to see if I could save some of my things. I don't have a lot…well, less now, but I didn't have a lot and I didn't really want to lose any of it." She looked up at him. "There as a man on the steps as I was going up. He had blood on his shirt and…he was breathing but not awake. I pulled him down two flights of stairs before someone came and got him. Another firefighter. He was going to take me but leave him and I couldn't have that. Not for me."

"He would have died without your help. The other firefighters were already out of the building and hadn't been able to find him. The man who went in to get you had to go against his commander's orders to find his friend. He said he thought he saw someone go in and he had to check. It was you he saw, and you led him right to his friend." She waited for him to tell her that she was stupid for going in, but he only sat in the chair that Allen had been in. "What else?"

"He picked me up. The second one, he'd picked me up, but I couldn't leave the hurt guy there. So I made him carry him instead of me. I was supposed to hold onto his belt or something. But I couldn't for...." When Luke laughed, she glared at him. "He was just going to leave him there to die. After I'd carried him all by myself down those stairs, he was fucking going to live."

"He did. Dave Patrick is his name. He and his wife are expecting their first child in a few weeks. When he was coming down the stairs, he was hit by a beam that had fallen from the upper floors. He never knew what happened until a few days later, when he was told you saved his life. Needless to say, he's very grateful that you decided to be stupid." She wanted to take offense to him calling her stupid, but she'd done enough calling herself that when she'd been in the house. "You hit your head."

"Yes. When...I'm not sure if I fell and hit my head or I hit my head and fell. I was pretty dizzy by then and couldn't really think very well, much less breathe." She took a deep breath and smiled. "I guess it wasn't as bad as I thought, right?"

When he leaned back in the chair, she had a feeling he was keeping something from her. And as much as she hated secrets, she was pretty sure she didn't want to know whatever it was right now. If ever. When he didn't tell her, she felt her body tense up more for some reason. Jack wanted to run, get far away from him and whatever he had to say right now.

"Your lungs were burnt badly. They had you on a machine that helped you breathe, but you'd done so much damage to your lungs that they were beginning to shut down. All of your body was fighting just to help your breathing. Basically, you were not breathing on your own at all, and you were suffering from it." She nodded, very afraid. "The rest of your body was being used up because it was working so hard to keep oxygen flowing to your brain. When we got to the hospital, you were given less than a five-percent chance of surviving."

"Yet here I am." He nodded. "Why do I have the feeling that you know something I need to know? I'm not saying I want to know, just that you know it." She was babbling again and tried to slow her brain down, but all sorts of things were popping in and out, like a skipping record.

"I do. I'm just not sure how to tell you. If we hadn't done what we did, you'd be dead, not sitting there looking like sex on a stick on my bed." She shifted under the blanket and realized she was naked. "Yes, you are naked. As you know, all your things were burned up."

"Nobody had a shirt they could put on me?" She looked around the room slightly panicky, and he stood up. "Just don't touch me right now. I feel...I feel like one of those plants that dies if you touch it. Not a good way to put it, but right now I'm sort of...is it really loud in here? And bright? Is it really, really bright in here?" Her breathing seemed to be caught somewhere between her lungs and her nose. Nothing was moving; she was becoming really light-headed. Then suddenly her head was down and he was talking to her.

"Take a deep breath." He lifted her chin up to stare into her eyes. She was still trying to figure out how he'd gotten across the room so fast when he told her to breathe again.

"I'm fucking breathing. In fact, I swear I can hear your heart beating. Fuck, I'm stressing out here." She could feel her head begin to spin again, and she knew that she was losing it. Suddenly his mouth was taking hers.

The kiss…it was the best kiss she'd ever tasted, but the kiss was making her think things she'd not thought of in months, maybe even years. When he ran his tongue over her lips, she opened to let him in and grabbed his arms. He was devouring her. When he lifted his head, just a few scant inches from her, he looked down at her with the most amazing eyes. Jack wanted to moan, wanted to beg him to continue, but she could only stare at him.

"You taste delicious." She nodded and licked her lips to taste him there. "Jacklyn, I want to kiss you again. Would you mind?"

"No." Before she could form the rest of the sentence, like "but it's not a good idea," he was taking her again. This time it wasn't gentle or even soft, but a kiss that made her think he was hungry and she was the entire menu. Her back touched the pillow, and she felt him settle over her. Jack ran her hands down his back and felt his muscles ripple under her fingertips. He moaned when she dug her nails into him. Christ, the man was like holding onto a live wire.

"I want you." She wanted him as well and moaned when he cupped her breast. "I want to suckle you. I want to drink from you until you fill me with your cream."

It was all sounding great to her and she shifted beneath him to have him between her thighs. The moment his thick cock touched her clit, she cried out against his mouth as a small yet powerful climax left her wanting more. A great deal more.

"Please. I need you." He growled at her and she pulled him back to her breast. "Make me come again. I need it desperately. I need to come, please?"

He moved down her body, and she wanted to sob. He was leaving her, and she needed something from him.

When the blankets were pulled off her, she looked down at him as he lifted her leg up to his mouth. The moment he licked her calf, Jack laid back and closed her eyes.

"Watch me, Jacklyn. I want you to watch me while I feast on you." She lifted her body up enough to rest on her elbows. Christ, he was so close to her pussy that she lifted her hips up for him to take her. "Tell me what you want."

"Eat me." He nodded and ran his fingers over her hips. "You're killing me. Just do it so I can come. I've not had sex in an extremely long time, and right now I could slide my fingers in me and get off, but I have a feeling you're going to be much better. Will you show me? Please?"

Luke lay down between her legs again and she watched him. When he lowered his head to her pussy, she felt her entire body tense for what he was going to do. The moment he licked her clit, ran his tongue deep into her nether lips, Jack cried out another quick release that had her panting and begging him again.

Luke pulled her thighs wider apart and covered her entire pussy with his mouth. He ate at her like it was his last meal. Jack felt her climax rise again and curled her fingers into his hair to hold him to her when she did. When his fingers slid into her, fucking her with his tongue, Jack came so hard that she saw stars dancing behind her closed lids. Before she could catch her breath, he was climbing up her body, biting at her, and then licking the tiny wound with his tongue.

His cock was thicker than she'd ever seen, and he was spilling precum on her as he moved closer to her mouth again. All she could think about was him fucking her, taking her so hard that in the morning she'd be sore and not give a shit.

"I'm going to hurt you a little." She nodded, thinking that right now, she didn't care so long as he filled her. "Open for me, baby. I need to fuck you."

Opening her legs as wide as she could, he slid his cock just to the tip inside of her. Jack felt her pussy pull at him, and she rolled her hips up to take more of him in. When he chuckled a little, she looked up at him.

"Take me." He slammed forward, filling her up and taking her breath away. When he moved, sliding out then back in, Jack held him tightly because she knew that when they came—and there was no doubt that it was going to be very soon—it was going to be explosive. Wrapping her ankles around him, she felt his teeth graze over her throat to her shoulder. When he bit her, not hard but hard enough, she screamed out his name as her body detonated. And when he sank his teeth into her harder, the only thing she could think of was biting back. Pulling his shoulder to her mouth, Jack felt her teeth sort of shift in her mouth, and she sank them deeply into his hot skin. Blood filled her mouth and she realized how starved she was for the taste of him. Drinking it down, she came again when he lifted her ass up for harder thrusts.

When he came, roaring out her name, she came a second, then a third time when he threw back his head and howled. Jack fainted, her vision blurring and her body spent. She thought of the man she'd just had the most incredible sex she'd ever had with. Christ, she didn't even ask him for a condom.

~~~

Luke was afraid to move. He really wasn't even sure he could. Lifting his head, he looked down at Jacklyn. She was even more beautiful now that she was all mussed and swollen from him. He kissed her lip gently where a drop of blood was and knew that it was his. She'd bitten him. Not only had she bitten him, she'd claimed him as well. Luke felt as if he'd been given the best gift in the world. Now all he had to do was tell her what she'd done by making love with him.

Luke rolled to his back and pulled her over him. She was warm, like all weres were, and she fit him like a nice warm blanket. When she shifted, positioning herself between his legs, Luke felt his cock thicken again at the thought of taking her. He glanced down her body and saw her lovely ass and cupped her to him. She moaned and moved again. This time her pussy wrapped around his cock. He either had to get up, wake her up, or take her again. She lifted her head and looked at him.

"Do you know that we didn't use protection?" Luke nodded. "I won't even go into the fact that I have no idea where I am, who you are, or how the hell I got here. Is that something you could share with me before I get up and ride you?"

"I'd rather you rode me." He rocked her over his cock and watched her need fill her face. "If you ride me right now, I'll tell you whatever you want to know."

She rolled her hips twice, and he pulled her leg up so that he could slide into her. She rocked forward in a slow canting-like move until he couldn't take it any longer. Rolling her to her back again, he held her hip while he fucked her.

"You said I could ride you." He moved his hand down her ass to her tight hole. "What are you going to — ?" She cried out when his finger entered her.

"Come for me like this and I'll let you ride me as hard as you want." She nodded and he moved his finger in and out of her as he did his cock. She was panting hard and holding onto him when he rolled to his back. "Come on me, Jacklyn. I want to watch you take your pleasure."

She moved over him, never letting his cock go. When her thighs were on either side of him, she dug her fingers into his chest and bucked over him. Luke held onto her hips, not to slow her but to keep himself from taking over. He could see the enjoyment on her face, and it made him want to give her whatever she wanted.

Sitting up when she leaned back, he took first one breast then the other into his mouth, just nibbling on the tips until she held him to her. When the ride seemed to be out of sync, he rolled her over again and pounded deep. Jacklyn cried out when he bit down on her shoulder again, and he felt her tighten around him in a hard climax. Luke came with her, filling her body with his seed even as she bit into him again. Christ, he didn't know who was more aggressive right now, but he was certainly loving it. This time he knew that he wasn't going to be able to move for a long time. Sleep took him like a storm moving over the grass in the summer.

Luke woke when he heard a door shut. He sat up, thinking that someone was attacking him, and Jacklyn froze in mid-step coming from the bathroom. Luke lay back down, relieved. She didn't sit on the bed but moved to the chair. He pulled the pillows behind his head and shoulders and sat up.

"You could come back to bed." She shook her head and he noticed that she had on one of his shirts. "When we leave here, I'll have Slone lend you something to wear. She's little like you are."

"And Slone would be...?" He wanted to laugh, but she looked like a jealous bitch, a she-bitch, and he thought it was not the time to test the old saying that mates couldn't hurt each other.

"She's my sister-in-law. She's married to my older brother." She nodded and sat back in the chair. "Come here."

"No. If I get back into that bed, we'll never talk. And as much as I'd like to fuck you again, I don't think that's going to get me the answers I need. So you know, I don't ever do this. Have sex with perfect strangers."

"You think I'm perfect?" She rolled her eyes. "I was glad that you decided to break your habit with me. If you come here, I'll show you just how glad I am."

"Quit stalling. Tell me, and if you think that beating around the bush is going to win you favor, it's not. I'm sated for now. And that's not to say I'm going to have sex with you again, but right now, you have a better chance of not pissing me off overly much than you would have had before." He nodded. "Start with why am I here."

"As I said, you were dying, and in order to save you, it was better if we could do it in private. I had to...what do you know about paranormals?" She eyed him hard, and he watched her face. "You know a few."

"I know one. At least I think I know one. He said that he's not, but I swear I saw him change into something to save my stupid ass." She stood up and started to pace, and Luke started to tell her she was distracting him when she walked in front of the window. The sun shining through his shirt gave him a perfect view of her lovely body. "Are you listening to me? Or is your mind on sex again?"

"Sex." She huffed, and he grinned. "You asked. But what is he? I mean, is he a shifter or a vampire?"

"There are vampires too?" He nodded, and she sat again. "A wolf. He changed into a wolf, though he denied it. One night when I was working late he came outside when I was…when someone was trying to rape me. He changed and the man ran away. And one other time there was…this is going to sound really stupid, but I swear a large tiger was chasing me through the building. It took me over an hour to lose her."

"She let you go. She could have found you whenever she wanted by your scent. I'll show you sometime when we play out in the woods." He watched her as she absorbed this. "Tell me what you're thinking."

"You said when we play. And don't…I'm not ready for you to explain that yet, but what would you be when we go out to play?" He wanted to get up and hold her. He could see she was beginning to put the pieces together but she wanted to do it on her own.

"I'm a wolf too. And I'm assuming that the other wolf you know is Max." She nodded and started to walk around the room. She picked up two small decorative things and put them back before she stood in front of the window again. Luke talked quietly to give her time to think. "I'm the second son of six men. All of us are werewolves. My father—you'll meet him later—is also a wolf. As is my sister-in-law, Slone."

"And so am I." He told her yes even though she'd not asked. "This was done because I was dying and it was the only way to save me. I'm assuming that you did this to me and that Allen had some part in it."

"It was and he did." She still stared out the window, and he felt his heart hurt for her. "You're only alive because I was able to convert you quickly. When you changed, your body healed completely, including your lungs and the few burns you had."

"Can you change me back?" He told her no. "Then what am I supposed to do now? I mean, I have a life as a person. I'm not saying this like I'm ungrateful or anything, but I have no desire to be a werewolf for the rest of my life."

"You can still have the same life, Jacklyn. You're not anything less than you were before, but more of everything. And you can stay here with me." She shook her head. "Jacklyn, I didn't just save your life, but I saved you for me. You're my—"

"It's just Jack. Not Jacklyn, just Jack. And don't say it." He snapped his mouth closed. He was frustrated with her and with himself. He needed to tell her what she was doing there. "I want you to make arrangements for me to get back to my place. I'm well aware that it's gone, but I need to start my life like this."

"You're my mate." She shook her head. "The moment you and I had sex, the second you bit me when you came, we bonded and mated. You and I are a couple. We will stay together until we die. I'm your other half the same as you are to me. We're a couple."

"No. I'm not your anything. It was great sex. The best I've ever had and more than likely will ever have, but I'm not spending my life with you as a wolf. I don't know how I'm going to get this fixed, but I am." He stood up and she backed away. "Bullying me won't change my mind. And you need to cover up. I don't know where I am, but I'm going to see about staying somewhere that's not your room."

"Good luck with that." He left her standing there and went into the bathroom. He stared at himself in the mirror, then slammed his fist into his reflection. Turning on the shower, he stepped into the cold water and let it run over him until he was chilled to the bone. His body now matched the condition of his heart. Frozen.

Chapter 5

Jack had no idea where she was, of course, but had a feeling that below her, down the big staircase, was going to be a way out. But what she didn't expect—and once she thought of it she should have—was to find several people standing in the first room she entered. They stopped talking the moment she walked in, and she knew they were talking about her.

"I pissed off Luke. I don't really care, but if this is his house, he might be inclined to toss you all out." A beautiful woman came forward and handed her a pair of pants. After thanking her, she pulled them on. Jack had no idea why she felt comfortable with these people, but she did. "Where can I find a place to stay? I think you all might know my brother, Allen."

"We do. He's staying here for a few more days too. If you need him, I can find him for you." She shook her head at the older man. "Up to you, of course, but I know that he's been worried. I'm Cash Emerson by the way. This is my son and alpha, Hunter. His wife, Slone. This is Jarrett and Graham, my other sons. You'd be Jack Wagner."

"I would be. And Christ, you guys are huge, aren't you?" Cash laughed and she decided that she kind of

liked him, despite who his son was. "I really need to have
a place I can think. Here? I don't think I'm going to get to
do that the way I want. I need quiet and space."

"And what is it you have to think about?" She looked
at Slone, who sat down at the large table. "Please have a
seat. I'm tired a lot lately, and sitting is so much
friendlier."

"No offense, lady, but I don't really want to get too
friendly." The big man, Hunter, she thought his name
was, laughed. "You know a good joke? Because I gotta tell
you, I could use one about now."

"You've been very friendly with Luke. In fact, you've
bonded and mated with him." He grinned when she felt
her face heat up. "Allen said you like it straight. I'm
assuming that you still like your information that way."

"That guy, Luke? He said that too. Something about
biting during sex." Hunter nodded and Jack felt the need
to sit down. "I have no idea what that really means, but
I'm assuming that it's not going to get me out of here any
time soon. And I don't want to offend any of you, but I'm
fucking on edge right now."

"No, it's not going to get you out of here. Where you
go, I do. I've tried to explain that to you twice now." She
turned to see Luke standing there. Christ, he'd been
gorgeous naked; with a suit and tie on, he looked like she
could have him for breakfast, lunch, and dinner with a
few snacks in between. When he looked at her, she had a
feeling he knew just what she was thinking and lifted her
chin. He laughed as he reached for a glass in the cabinet
over the sink.

"I think there's been a mistake here." Jack tore her
eyes from Luke to look at Cash to speak to him. "I know
this was done to me to save me, but I'd really like to see

about getting me changed back. Not that I'm ungrateful or anything, but I don't want a lifestyle that includes changing into a big dog every month."

"We're not really dogs. Canines, yes, but not dogs. We're wolves. And so are you." Luke leaned against the counter and he sipped the tea as he continued. "I told you before, you're not going to be able to get back to just being human. You're my mate, as I've said, and we're bonded. We're going to have to talk about this sooner or later, Jack. You're a wolf. You're my mate and we're together."

"Fuck off. And in case you didn't get it, I don't have a place for you or me to go. Not that I want you with me, but you have to know that some people aren't cut out to be…what the fuck. I'm not going to explain myself to you again. I told you, I need a place to stay, and you are so not going to go—"

She was up and in his arms almost before she could finish the next word. When he turned and pressed her against the counter he'd been leaning against, she felt his cock thicken and stretch. Moaning, she held onto him as he rocked into her several more times before he stepped back. Her body was screaming for him to take her and then she remembered they were not alone. Before she could think, Jack slapped him hard across the face. And when she drew back to slap him again, he grabbed her hand and held it.

"Once was quite enough to make your point." He let her go but didn't move back. And even though there were several inches between them, she had a feeling he could close that distance in a heartbeat. "I have to go to work today. And I need to get you something to wear."

"I don't want your charity." Her face heated again when someone behind him cleared their throat. "I really hate you right now. You're nothing but a bully and a prick. You could be a good deal nicer to me. I've been through a lot."

"So you have. But you didn't think so when I was fucking you." She stared at him as he turned and left her standing there. If she usually had a quick comeback—and she always prided herself on having one—this time she was speechless. Tears filled her eyes and she looked blurrily at the people around the room before excusing herself and leaving. Going out the same door that Luke had, she saw him pulling away. Not that she wanted to talk to him, but she was somewhat...hurt, she thought, that he'd just leave her when she was pissed.

Moving to the tree line, she realized that she should have borrowed a pair of shoes, but was too pissed to go and ask for a pair. There was a dusting of snow on the ground and she had no jacket either. But she wasn't cold. On the contrary, she was quite warm. Moving deeper into the trees, she let the tears fall. Jack hated whiners and despised it more when she was the one doing it. Finding the open water behind the big house, she sat on the cool bank and looked out over the water.

A wolf. She was a wolf. Thinking about that depressed her, so she thought about what she was giving up to be one. That didn't help her mood at all. Just as she was contemplating jumping into the water and letting it take her away, she heard something snap beside her. She looked up at Slone as she sat down.

"I nearly drowned in this water a long time ago. While I don't recommend you diving in, I have been where you are right now." Jack had a feeling that she wasn't just talking about the side of the fast moving river. "It's a bit overwhelming, huh?"

"A bit." She stared out at the water and the occasional tree that went floating down as well. "I lost everything. I don't know about my job, which if I really think about it, it really wasn't much of one anyway. But my car is gone, my clothing, computer, my piece of shit television. I even lost what little things from my childhood that I managed to save over the years. And now? Now I'm not even the same person I was before. Oh, let's not forget that I'm mated, whatever the hell that means, to a man that I don't care for but love having sex with. Did I miss anything?"

"No, I think you about covered it. You're not, you know. Not the same person, but an improved one. Not the same but better in a great many ways." Slone leaned back, and Jack noticed that she, too, was barefooted. "You're going to notice a lot of things that are going to give you a better quality of life. You'll heal much quicker than before. Smell things you never gave a thought about before this. You'll also find a person within yourself that you never knew was there. The stronger version of yourself. But I'm thinking now you might have found her a long time ago."

"I'm not someone men or women want as friends. So I've been very good at shoving them away so I don't let myself be hurt. Or hurt them." Jack leaned back too but lay on her back. "My brother? Someone said he gave the permission needed to change me into this. Do you know why he was contacted at all?"

"I'm sorry, but I don't. I would assume that somewhere along the line you gave them something that would have made them search for him. You needed to be converted or you would be dead now. What he did was save you." Jack didn't say anything, and Slone seemed to be content to not speak either.

"I know about you. Not a great deal, but I know about you. When I'd get post cards from Allen, he'd mention you. I know that I don't talk to him, but I still look out for him. I did some research." Slone didn't speak, and Jack turned to look at her. "I really like the way you took care of that other mayor. The way you've helped the people in this town, especially my brother. Thank you for that."

"I didn't help your brother. He did whatever it is he's done all on his own. Luke likes him and that alone is enough for the rest of us to like him." Jack nodded and turned to look at the sky again as Slone continued. "I know about you too. It's within my powers to search you as well."

"Whatever you found out, it's more than likely true. I didn't, however, leave my brother in jail to rot, as he accused me of some time ago. I simply knew that if I didn't stop when I did, he'd be dead and me with him." Slone said something low, but Jack wanted to explain herself before she kicked her to the curb. "He was going down the wrong path and at the fast rate he was going, he'd have been hitting the bottom within days, not years. I had to distance myself from him or slip in with him. Plus, there was our father. He's a piece of shit and I hope I never see him again."

"Allen said that he's not a nice man and that your mother died when he was young." Jack snorted but didn't say anything. "Allen did what he had to do. He told us all that you'd hate him for it, but he had to repay you in some way for what you did for him."

"For what?" Slone said she had no idea. "I left him in a cell with several other criminals. My father, he called me for nearly a month to come and give Allen money to get him straightened out, but I didn't. I'm so broke now that the thought of trying to purchase anything I might need is terrifying. Getting my car here is a daunting idea, and other than sleeping in my car when or even if I ever get it here, it's doubtful that I'd make it through one night without someone killing me in it. My life is really fucked up right now."

"You have a home with Luke." She shook her head, and Slone laughed. "Your boss called here. He found out from someone that you'd been hurt. You've been fired. I'm sorry."

"Figures." Jack felt so depressed that the river was looking better and better all the time. "I hated that job anyway. I love what I can do, but the guy I worked for was an idiot and a fool. He would take on clients without getting any idea what they wanted. One of them wanted us to use mentally handicapped people in an ad to show how easy their twist-off lids of soup worked. They wanted me to use the phrase 'even a retard could do it.'"

"Oh my goodness." Jack felt her temper rise when she thought of those people. "And what did your boss say about their ad campaign? Plenty, I hope."

"Yeah, he had plenty to say, all right. Most of which was directed at me for not doing what the client wanted. Can you imagine the feedback the firm would have gotten? Christ, people would have been picketing us for months." Jack sat up as a large island of trees floated by them. Near it, swimming right beside it, was a man in a wet suit. Before she could ask about it, Slone laughed.

"That would be Graham. He's another of Luke's brothers. He graduates from college in a few months and he is doing some extra work on the river."

They watched as he slid from the water to the other shore, and Jack thought about how much better Luke looked. Then she flushed.

"Luke is a good man," Slone said softly.

"I'm sure he is. But I don't want him any more than I want to be a wolf." She turned to her then. "There is no way I can get changed back, is there? I'm going to be part animal for the rest of my life."

"No, I'm afraid not." Slone didn't continue for some time and for some reason Jack enjoyed it. She was never one to prattle on and on about nothing, and sitting here next to this woman, she found that she liked her, just a little.

"I have some money in the bank. Not a great deal, but enough that it will give me a start somewhere so long as it was really cheap and had furniture and a really low to zero deposit on the thing. Then I'd have enough left over to buy some underwear and a nice big bottle of shampoo and soap and stuff." Slone didn't answer so Jack continued. "As for my job, it's probably just as well he fired me. Sooner or later he would have anyway. I didn't play well with him wanting to fuck me every time he was near me. And his wife was a real bitch about me not sucking off—not up to, but off—her husband. What kind of people are they? I used to wonder. Now? Well, I suppose it matters very little anymore."

"Wolves are very possessive. And so you know, Luke will kill him if he tries anything like that again. I'm not sure Luke won't want to even now. Like I said, very possessive." Jack turned to Slone and asked her why he'd care. "You're his mate. And as you have very little experience with us, then I'll tell you now that wolves, especially when it comes to their mates, are very protective too. They will kill if necessary to keep you from harm."

"I don't want, nor do I need, his help. I've been doing just fine on my own." Jack felt her temper rise. "And the first time he goes all macho shit on me, I'll show him just how much I can take care of myself."

Slone laughed, and Jack turned to her. She thought it sounded like music. Not bells, as she'd heard it described in books she sometimes read, but more like small cymbals, the kind that people wore on their fingers. Before she could tell her anything more, a large wolf came out of the woods and stared at them both.

"Is he going to eat me?" Slone stood up and laughed. As she moved away, she said over her shoulder that it was Luke, and if she wanted him to, he'd probably be thrilled. Jack turned back to the big dark wolf and stared at him. "I thought you had to go to work."

You've made it difficult to get anything done, so I came here to run. She was surprised to have him speak to her in her mind, but he continued before she could ask him how he did that. *Why don't you shift for me and we'll run? Then when you're deep enough in the woods, I'll take you to the ground and fuck you and your animal.*

"No." She started to stand up, but he stood over her. She could feel his breath on her cheek when he nudged her shoulder. Every part of her body tensed, but it wasn't from fear. She was as sexually aroused as she'd ever been. "Step back."

Take off your clothes for me. My wolf, he wants to taste his mate. Her body seemed to have heated everywhere, especially between her legs. When he shifted on his feet and buried his nose in her crotch, instead of pushing him away, Jack found herself opening her legs wider for him.

Let him taste your pussy. Let him lap at you until you come down his throat. Then I'll do the same. Eat you until you scream out my name.

"He can't want to taste me. I'm a person." Luke growled low, and she moaned. "This is sick. Animals don't have sex with humans." But the more she lay there with his head between her legs, the wetter she could feel herself getting. Finally, she lay back and bent her knees and opened her legs wider. The big wolf nipped at her so hard she came, and she had to have more.

Taking off her pants was hard. The wolf wouldn't move back, and every time he touched the skin she uncovered, he nipped at her. She was panting, almost as hard as he was, when she was naked from the waist down. As soon as she lay back, the wolf buried his mouth over her and entered her with his tongue. Jack came screaming and holding onto his fur so tightly that she was sure she'd hurt him. But he continued to eat her through two more of the most earth shattering climaxes she'd ever had. Then Luke was suddenly there.

He didn't say a word as he lowered his head to her pussy. His tongue circled her clit twice before he suckled it hard. She screamed again as he slid his fingers into her. Jack was riding his mouth and hand so hard that she was surprised that he didn't get bucked off. Then he started up her body, leaving her wanting, and her need so profound that she was sobbing for him to take her.

Nothing could have prepared her for the way her body reacted to him entering her. She felt his cock, thick and long, move into her sheath as if he were filling her. She'd had sex before but nothing, no man, had filled her like he was. And it wasn't just her pussy but her entire body.

"This doesn't change anything." He laughed as he ripped his shirt off her and took her nipple, just the tip, into his mouth. As he fucked her, slow, long strokes, she wrapped her legs around his waist and rose up to meet each of his downward slides. She couldn't believe she needed to come after the amazing climaxes she'd just had.

"Come for me, love. Wrap your sheath tightly around me and milk my cock of all my seed." He didn't order her to come but begged her. She felt her body bow up off the ground and simply come apart for him. As soon as he bit into her shoulder, she came again and sank her own teeth into him. He roared out his release even as he pounded into her, his cum hot as it splashed deep inside of her. Jack knew that for as long as she lived, this would be a memory that she'd hold close to her. She had no idea why, but she just knew that it would.

~~~

He had to walk naked back to where he'd entered the woods. Jack had left him in a huff, but all he could think about was how much he'd needed her, and how much she'd seemed to need him. Luke was pulling his jacket over his head when Hunter spoke to him through their link.

Your mate is here. And she's pissed off. What the hell did you do to her? Luke didn't answer, but Hunter seemed to have understood. *Ah. I see. And during this time in the woods, you never thought to tell her that you had clothing sent for her.*

Fuck. Hunter laughed again. *She's going to be pissed even more when she finds out that I've ordered more for her and that it'll be delivered today. Do you think you could tell her for me?*

He didn't expect Hunter to do it and wasn't surprised when he told him hell no. He thought about his dad but decided against that. His father was a great man and a huge flirt. Luke didn't know how he'd feel if his mate liked his dad more than she did him. And right now, Luke knew that she pretty much hated him.

I don't know what do to. Hunter said he understood his frustrations. *What am I supposed to do with her? The sex is fucking fantastic and she seems to enjoy it. Christ, does she enjoy it; but that's all we have right now. I don't know what to do with her or for her.*

It's enough for now. Luke didn't think so but got into his car to drive back to the office. He'd been gone much longer than he'd expected, but it had been worth it. *But she does need to get this settled in her mind that she's a wolf forever. She asked Slone if it was true. She told her it was, but Slone didn't think she believed her. Perhaps you two could...I don't know, date or something.*

Date? They had been having sex like they had been starved for it for decades. He thought they should go out on a date now? Luke started to tell him it was a stupid idea when he thought of seeing her all dressed up and all his.

Where would you suggest we go? His brother told him he couldn't do everything for him. *I guess...what if I took her to her hometown? Maybe pick up her car, see about her job or something.*

Oh that reminds me. You remember Dan's dad, Max? Well, he apparently knows Jack. Worked in her building where she worked for that advertising firm. He has something for her. Luke felt his wolf snarl at him but held him back. *He said he'd like to talk to her if you don't mind. And I'd like to suggest that you let him. It might go a long way for her and you if you*

*don't go all ape shit, as Slone is so fond of calling it when I get a
little possessive of her.*

My wolf is already ape shit. Hunter laughed. *I'll tell her,
if you don't mind. And let Max know that it's okay with me if it
is with her. And I'll try my best not to go stupid with him.*

Luke made his way to work. He wasn't in the best of
humor still, but at least he was getting some things done.
As soon as he pulled into his space behind the courthouse,
he seriously gave a good deal of thought to just going
back home, finding Jack, and making love to her all day.
But instead, he got out and went inside.

"There are a number of things that need your
attention first thing." Luke stared at Allen and nearly did
turn to go back. "You have two meetings with—"

"Who hit you?" Luke knew that his wolf surfaced,
and when Allen stepped back from him, he felt bad. "I'm
sorry. But please tell me who beat the shit out of you. And
where else are you hurt?"

"I'm fine." But he wasn't. As soon as he started to
walk away, Luke knew that maybe a few ribs were broken
as well. "You have a lot of meetings this morning."

Luke didn't move. He knew that if he stood there long
enough, either he'd shift and go find who hurt his new
friend or Allen would simply tell him. When he turned to
look at him, Luke knew it was going to be him telling
what happened.

"I was coming out of the building yesterday after you
left. I only went to get some lunch, I swear. But they
jumped me. I'm not sure who they all were, but one was
Danny. That guy who got you arrested." Luke told him to
continue as he sat down on the chair in the hall. "They
said that it was my fault that Conklin was in jail and that

I'm the reason things are going to shit here. I tried to tell them that it was him, but—"

"But they didn't want to hear it." Allen nodded. "How bad is it? And don't tell me again that you're fine. I can smell your pain and hear how hard you're breathing."

Luke couldn't actually smell his pain, but Allen didn't know that. When he sat down on the edge of the desk, Luke knew it was going to be worse than he thought. Allen lifted his shirt and Luke cursed.

"I think I have a couple of broken ribs. And my leg hurts like a fucker." Allen blushed. "Sorry. I tried taking some over the counter stuff, but it doesn't even touch the pain. I got more on my back, but I can't see them. I have a feeling they're just as colorful."

Luke stood up, took his briefcase and jacket to his office, and came out to see that Allen hadn't moved. Helping him to the elevator, he spoke to him as calmly as his wolf would allow. Luke was fucking pissed, and his wolf...well, he wanted blood, and a good deal of it.

Chapter 6

Hunter searched for nearly ten minutes before he found Jack. He should have known she'd be outside. Every time she wasn't with his wife, she was out of doors. Hunter sat down next to her at the little patio table they'd bought this past summer.

"Your brother has been hurt." She stood up and then sat down again. "I'm to take you to the hospital —"

"Drugs?" Hunter shook his head. "Is he…is he dead? Please tell me…you said hospital, not morgue, so I can only hope he's still alive. Right? He's still alive?"

"He's been beaten up. Not life threatening, but he is in a great deal of pain. I don't know all the particulars yet, as Luke just asked me to see if you wanted to come to the hospital." She nodded. "Honey, he's going to be all right. And Luke will make sure that whoever is responsible will not be."

She sat there for a long moment, not moving, not speaking. Hunter had an overwhelming urge to take her into his arms like a child, simply give her some comfort. He knew that he couldn't, that Luke would tear him up, but he did reach for her hand and wasn't really surprised that she pulled her hand back. Allen did the same thing, not really seeking or needing a touch for comfort like most humans did.

"I don't know much about Allen any more. Just what Cash and your other brothers have told me." She didn't move to get dressed, and he waited. Hunter knew she was hurting, not just from this but with all the changes in her life. "My father called me today too. I don't know how he got your number, so if you have to change it, I'll pay."

"We're working through that now. It's a new number and public, so if he knew where Allen or you were staying, he could have gotten it." She nodded and still sat. "Do you want me to take you to Allen?"

"He hates me." That shocked Hunter, but before he could tell her that Allen worshiped her, she continued. "I did leave him to rot in that jail cell. I'd had it with him and Dad. He was spoiled as a child, and when Mom died...when she died, it was as if everything fell apart and they both decided that I'd take her place. I spent so much of my life catering to them. So much of my own money to bail them both out of one jam or another. And even though my father had a great deal of money from my mom's estate, he never spent his when mine was right there for the taking. And take he did. I couldn't have a life while trying to live up to the one that they expected me to give them. I just needed my space. And now...now I live with people I don't know, without a single penny to my name. I don't mean to whine really, and I know that it's all that I do, but I feel so...pressured. Like everything is falling down around me and I can't keep it up any longer."

"Jack, you have a lot here if you'd just let us help you with it. Luke will care for you. He did mess up with buying you all those things without talking to you, but he meant well." She nodded, and that's when he noticed that she was wearing a pair of his wife's pants and another of Luke's shirts. He'd bet anything she'd not touched a single thing in those bags. "Why don't you go and get dressed? I'll take you into town, and you can see that Allen is all right. He did ask for you."

She turned and looked at him, and Hunter saw for the first time what all this, everything, was costing the young woman. Jack looked haunted, depressed even. When he started to speak again, she turned away.

"I'll go in. I...I have to make some arrangements to get my own car. And a few other things from my desk at work." He nodded, but he knew that both of those things had been taken care of. "I'll need a ride back too. Do you think you could lend me a car for a few days? Or a bike? I don't care."

"I'll see what I can do for you." She nodded and stood up. When she entered the house, he felt his heart break for her. Pulling the small notepad toward him, he looked at the drawing she'd been doing. Christ, it was amazing. Picking it up, he went to find Slone. This was something she needed to see.

"She did this? This morning?" He nodded at Slone. He could tell by her face that she was just as excited as he was. "This looks just like what we've been looking for. Did you tell her?"

"No. I didn't even tell Luke, so he didn't tell her either." They both stared at the drawing of the store front that was going to be their antique shop. The old chair, watering can, and the quilt lying over an old table were beautiful. There was even a small dog sleeping in front of the rocker and flowers just on the edge of the page. There was no writing on it, of course. She'd not known about the name they'd picked out, but it was just exactly what they'd been looking for.

"We have to tell her." They both turned when the door behind them opened and Hunter smiled at Jack. When she took a step back, he had to laugh. She was just like her brother in that she was very distrusting. "Why did you draw this?"

He sounded too excited, his voice maybe just a little hard. When she took another step back, he sat down. Hunter looked at Slone for help.

"This is beautiful. And what my overbearing husband is trying to tell you, while scaring you shitless, is that we needed a drawing like this. For our business cards. What we'd like to know is why did you draw this particular thing?" Jack shrugged and put her hands in her pockets. It was then that Hunter realized she was embarrassed by their excitement.

"You're an amazing artist. I can see now why you worked in advertising. You must have had customers beating down your door." Again the shrug but still nothing. Then it hit him. "They didn't see it, did they? Christ, didn't they see what kind of work you could do for them? How much money you could have brought in for them?"

"When I was hurt...fired, I guess, I was working on a campaign for adult diapers. They were going to get sued for the work they wanted me to do. Not by my fault with the campaign, but with the company itself. The name of the company that we had and the structure of the packaging were so close to the name brand it was going to come back and bite them in the ass. Adult diapers they called them, nothing slick about that. Yet they had to have it called that. And the owners wanted me to make it sexy.

I'm pretty sure you can see where that was nearly impossible." She sat down and looked at them both. "You can use it if you want. Consider it payment for letting me stay here. In fact, if you have anything else you want drawn up, I can help you out. It would be nice to work again."

"Can you help me?" Hunter looked at Ellis when he came into the kitchen. "I want a fresh look. I don't want girly, but something that isn't the same old same old. The jackhammer is on about fifty other construction company logos."

"Sure." She looked at Hunter before nodding to Ellis. Hunter wondered if she realized that she'd done it. As his pack member, she was already understanding that he had to approve projects that were in his domain. Not that he would have kept her from it, but it was good to know she was a part of their pack.

"I have Emerson Builders. It's been in my family for a few generations. My dad's dad started it, and then Dad took it from him. Up until a few months ago, Hunter ran it. Then I took it when he became alpha." Hunter handed Jack the pad again and she tore off the drawing and handed it to him. They watched her sketch notes on a fresh page, and she drew a truck that looked just like the one that was currently parked in the drive. It had everything but the current logo on it.

"I have to go to the hospital now. My brother is hurt. But maybe this will give you an idea what I can do for you." Ellis asked if he was all right. "I don't know yet. Mr. Emerson said that he was fine, just beat up. I sort of...I was telling him that Allen and I aren't very close, and I've kind of decided that I'd like to rectify that. If he'll let me."

She continued to draw out things with the notes she'd made. Hunter watched as a building took shape, then a crew of men. The large truck with the name blazing across it in sharp lettering came to life. As it continued to take shape, Hunter noticed that Jack seemed to fade out, almost, he thought, like she was the only one there. When she laid down her pencil, she turned and handed the pad to Ellis.

"It's just a rough draft. If you have a better idea, I can do pretty much anything. I won't do trademarks; that's nasty business. So if that's the route you want to go, then count me out." She stood up and Ellis continued to stare at the pad. "It'll have to be bigger, any drawing you want. Bigger gives you more detail, better perspective, and you can even add—"

Ellis grabbed her into his arms and swung her around the room twice before he put her down. Usually so quiet and reserved, he looked alive. Hunter smiled too, just knowing that his brother was this happy. And Jack looked like she'd like to crawl into a hole and stay there. It might have been funny if not for it being so sad too.

"I love it. Christ, I love it. Do you...? You have no idea how much...this is simply...you're perfect." He hugged her again. "Can you draw this bigger, like you said? And stationary...I'll need it on billings, the truck. We'll have signs made. And I can have tee-shirts done up. I can't...." He hugged her again as he pulled out his cell phone. Jack looked at him with a look of complete confusion on her face.

"It was just a little thing. Not worth all that." Hunter laughed and so did Slone. "You guys are nuts. Just nuts."

Hunter was still laughing as he made his way out to the car with her. Slone was coming with them, as she had to see about some other things in town. He wondered when they could go baby shopping, but didn't ask. She was still getting used to that too.

Slone was doing so much better now about getting out in the public. Not to say she still didn't get scared and nervous, but she was making great headway into getting over things. And with Jack there, he could see her getting more and more public. He was going to love having Jack around just for that alone.

Luke was in the emergency room when they got there. Hunter watched Luke take Jack into his arms, then stiffen. She pulled back and shivered, there was fear there. When Hunter put his hand on Luke's shoulder, he could feel his wolf.

"Someone...." Hunter nodded. "Ellis should know better. I know he should. What the hell was he doing?"

"He hugged her. She did him a massive favor and he was happy." Hunter watched as Slone took Jack to the nurse's desk. "Calm him down or so help me, I'll do it for you. He was happy. He asked her for a favor and she did it. I don't even think he thought about what he was doing."

"What kind of favor?" He told him about the drawing and showed him the one she'd done for him. "She did this? I knew she worked for an advertising firm, but I had...this is really good. Damned good."

"You should see what she did for Ellis. He came in and asked for something fresh for the construction company, and she tossed a drawing off like it was nothing. You should have seen him. He was beside himself with excitement. Again, I don't even think he thought about what he was doing. I've never seen him so excited. Christ. She's that good." Luke nodded and turned to look at the woman. "You frightened her. Do something."

"What? I'm open for any and all suggestions on this. I'm at a loss about everything with her. Was it like this with Slone? I can't remember it being this hard with her." Luke turned back to him. "I have no idea what do to. She's depressed. I can almost taste it, she's so sad. I try to talk to her and she shuts me out. I think…damn it Hunter, I don't know what to do. Or even where to begin to help her. I've even suggested that she find a doctor and she cried. Cried. I finally had to leave the house. It was tearing me apart."

"I'm sorry." And he was. Hunter had no idea what to do. Jack was a wolf and she didn't want to be. She'd been made without her permission or knowledge, and it was hurting her. Plus to find out that she had a mate, one like his brother, would be a lot for anyone. Luke was a good man, but he seemed to be in over his head right now.

"How about I have Dad talk to her?" Luke nodded but continued to watch Jack. "Are you in love with her?'

"With all my heart." As he walked away, Hunter reached for their dad. He said that he'd come there right now after Hunter told him what was going on.

He's in love with her. And he's at a loss as to how to help her. His dad said he knew that Luke loved her, but he'd do his best to help her.

Poor thing. She just needs a little push is all. We'll get her there. And Hunter had to agree. She was going to need all the help she could get. And he decided that he'd look into her dad, too. He had a feeling there was something there as well.

~~~

Allen heard someone open the door and moaned. If someone poked him again, he was going to scream. He fucking hurt and they were making him hurt more. But when he turned his head to tell them, beg whoever it was to go away, he looked at his sister.

"You look lovely." Her face brightened to stain her cheeks and he felt his own face heat up. "I'm sorry. It's just...the last time I saw you...it wasn't very pretty."

"I guess not." She sat down and Allen didn't know what to say to her. "Hunter said you'd been beat up. I'm really sorry, but my first thought was that you'd gotten into some bad drugs. I shouldn't have thought that after you told me you were clean. I'm sorry."

Allen felt his heart twist in his chest for giving her reason to think that. "Thank you for that. But I was beaten up as I was coming out of work. I didn't see them until I was already down. But I don't blame you for thinking the worst of me. I wasn't a good person then."

"I didn't mean to leave you." He nodded and tried his best to stop the tears. Men didn't cry, according to his father, and old habits were hard to break. "I wasn't in a good place either. And you were tearing me apart with all the carelessness you were doing to yourself. I should have...I don't know what I could have done, but staying wasn't going to help either of us."

"Dad didn't help." She looked away, and he looked at her, really looked at her. "You look like Mom. Not exactly, but enough to know you're her daughter. I never noticed that before. But then it's been a long time since I've had a chance to look at you." He smiled when she turned to him again. And he could see his dad there too, the set of her chin, the way her hair seemed to be in the proper place all the time. He didn't tell her that, of course, but kept that bit of news to himself. He thought he'd live longer.

"Too long, I'm thinking." He smiled at her again. "Dad called me at Mr. Emerson's house. He said that he's coming here, for both of us. He told me that I owed him and that you did as well. What do you suppose he means by that? Not that I have anything for him right now, but he did say that."

"I don't know." A nurse came in and told him they were going to take him down to x-ray in a bit then left them again. "Will you stay? I mean, I know you have lots of things to do, and —"

"What am I going to do as a wolf?" Allen started to tell her she was alive but she spoke first. "I'm a dog, Allen. A big one with huge teeth. And no matter what I do, for the rest of my life, this thing is going to be inside of me. I can feel her. Moving inside of me like something monstrous. What am I supposed to do?"

"Live." She shook her head. "Jack, you had to live. If not for you, then for me. When Luke told me that you'd been hurt and that you might not make it, all I could think about was all the things I never got to tell you. All the wonderful things I didn't know about in your life. I wanted to thank you for what you did. Tell you that no matter what, you washing your hands of me was the best thing that could have happened to me."

"But I left you there." Allen nodded. "I didn't even answer any of your cards, never once acknowledged you in any way. I...I was so afraid you'd hurt me again."

"I wouldn't have. I never will again. I promise." He reached for her hand, and she took his. "I love you, Jack. You're my sister, all the family...all the family that I want or need. And I do need you to live for us so we can be there for each other."

90

They sat there until the nurse came back and she asked Jack if she wanted to go with him. Allen wanted her there. He was terrified that she'd just leave him again. And when she said she'd go, he squeezed her hand as they made their way down the hall. Luke was waiting near the x-ray room when they got there. He didn't look all that happy, and Allen glared at him as best he could with a swollen face.

"I know she's your mate and all." Luke nodded and frowned. "And you have to know that I respect you more than any man I've ever known. But if you hurt her, even to make her cry, I'll kill you."

Luke only stared at him for several seconds before he looked at Jack. Allen saw the change almost immediately and it occurred to him, just like that, that Luke Emerson loved his sister. Before either of them said anything else, he was pushed into the room to be examined. And for the first time in a very long time, Allen thought that things were going to be looking up. Not perfect, but certainly looking up.

By the time he was put back on the gurney, Allen was sweating. He'd never been twisted into so many shapes in his life. And he was pretty sure that he'd screamed at one point. Looking for his sister as soon as he came out, he was nearly sobbing with disappointment at her not being there. But Luke was.

"She had to go to the bathroom. I told her that I'd make sure you knew, first thing." Allan nodded and reached for the man's hand. He wasn't really surprised when he took it, but he was at the strength of his hold. "You're going to be all right, Allen. I promise you this."

"I hurt." Luke nodded and he could see his sister coming toward them. "You love her, don't you? Love her very much?"

"I do." Allen closed his eyes and felt the weight of the world slide off his shoulders. And it was weight that he'd not realized he'd been holding until then. "I won't hurt her. I know you think I was upset, but not at her. My brother hugged her. Wolves are very possessive of their mate."

"I understand." He didn't really, but it hurt too much to think. "Do you think you could hit me? Really hard. Right now I hurt badly enough that I'd let your wolf hit me if it made the pain go away."

Luke laughed and he said something to a nurse. It was that voice again, the one he'd used to get the other one to move Jack here. Allen knew in a few minutes, if not sooner, he'd be sliding away on some drugs. As much as he didn't like them anymore, he knew that if he didn't get some soon, he was going to be sick. And throwing up with broken ribs wasn't fun at all.

He was taken to the same emergency room cubical, but this time he wasn't put onto the bed, but told that he was being transferred to a real one. The thought of moving again nearly had him begging to be left alone, but a nurse came in and told him she was going to give him something for pain. Jack moved out of her way but didn't leave him. He wasn't sure if he wanted her to see him cry, because he was going to. And soon if the drugs didn't kick in.

"I love you." The nurse grinned at him and he wondered if she'd let him hug her. But instead making a fool of himself, he held onto his sister's hand while the nurse worked on his other side.

"Tell him." Jack looked around and Allen knew that she was afraid for Luke to hear. "Tell him what Dad did to you. He has a right to know."

"No one does. And you should forget it too." Allen felt the drugs taking their toll on him and he wanted to tell them to stop, that the familiar high was going to be his undoing. But he looked at Jack hard.

"He does. He's a good man. You've no reason to fear him." Jack shook her head and he could see her tears. It broke at Allen and he wanted to tell her to forget it, but it was important to them both, her and Luke. "Tell him for me. If you never do another thing for me, please tell him."

"Please don't do this." He nodded and closed his eyes. He had to work very hard at getting them opened again, and he stared at his sister, trying to get her to come into focus again.

"If you don't, then I will have to. Dad is coming and you know what he'll do." He felt his eyes drifting shut and got one of them opened as he tried again. "He deserves to know. You did the best you could and now you need him to help you."

Allen drifted off. His body betrayed him and he felt it sliding away from him before he could beg Jack again. Luke would protect her, because he certainly couldn't. Not that he'd ever tried, but his father had a way about him that would make most men, human men, run for cover. He was a mean and horribly terrifying person. As his fingers lost their ability to hold onto her hand any longer, Allen tried again, but he wasn't sure his words even came out right. All he could think about was their dad was coming and he was going to ruin everything again.

Allen slipped into his happy place. A place where no one would bother him, no one could hit him. It was the reason he'd done so many drugs as a kid, then as an adult. No one could get to him here. It was a place all his own that he'd created to escape. But Allen had a feeling that there was going to be no escape this time, no matter how many drugs he might take. And this time, even where he was, he decided that he wasn't going to go away and let Jack take all the blame, all the hurt. This time he was going to be there for her even if it got him killed.

Chapter 7

Luke had heard them. Jack didn't want to tell him something, and Allen said he would if she didn't. Luke had no idea what it was, but he wanted her to tell him. He didn't like that Allen had to threaten her, but if she told him, he'd forgive the man just about anything. But the way she was sitting in the chair made him believe that he'd turn to stone before she said anything.

"He'll be all right." She nodded but said nothing more. "I talked to my brothers. I guess you're a big hit with them. Ellis said that you were going to make him famous."

"It wasn't that much." Luke nodded and smiled. She looked like she was going to tell him something else, but she only got up to walk around the room. Allen had been sleeping for nearly two hours now and the doctors said it would be another couple before he was awake. They had given him something more after they'd read the film. He shivered when he thought of what the doctor had told them.

"I don't know how that young man was up and about. He has eleven broken ribs and one of them was all the way through his lung." The doctor cursed a little under his breath. "And his leg. It looks like someone kicked him with a steel-toed boot. There is enough muscle damage done to him that I'm going to cast it to keep him off it. Whoever did this to him needs to be horsewhipped."

"I agree." Luke had already sent Lee to Allen's room, then his apartment, to look for anything that might have a scent on it. He knew one name and it was going to give him a great deal of pleasure showing the man just what he did to those who dared hurt his family. Ellis was keeping an eye on Danny of Osborne Construction as of right now. And Hunter was keeping a look out for Hank Granger.

Hank Granger was the chief of police, and the sooner he was taken care of, the sooner life could go on at a normal pace. Luke wanted normal. He wanted it almost as badly as he did his mate.

"Can I borrow some money?" Luke looked at Jack when she spoke. "I don't need a lot...well, I'm not really sure how much I need, but I want to get some paper and some pens and stuff. I need to...I told your brother that I'd do his logo. I don't have the proper equipment."

"You can have whatever you want." She shook her head. "I know you still don't want to be my mate, but I want to see that you have anything and everything you need."

"I don't know what I need." He had a feeling she was talking about more than just paper and such. "I was wondering if you'd ask Mr. Emerson if I could use a room. There's this one in the back of his house that has a lot of windows. I don't think he's using it right now."

Luke knew the room. His dad had said it would make a great studio and had even asked Slone what she'd used it for. She said that mostly she used the room as a green house in the winter months. It was one of the reasons that her and his dad had started on their own greenhouse. The two of them were having a blast.

"I'm sure that he won't mind." She nodded. "Jack, could you come with me tonight to find a house? I have three in mind, and I'd very much like to have you look at them with me."

"I don't know anything about houses. I've never even lived in one." He was surprised by that but didn't comment as she continued. "After my mom died, we lived in a trailer with my father. We had...I guess they'd be called houses, but it was really just two apartments built in the same building. Before that it was a townhouse that was in a high income neighborhood. But in the trailer, our neighbors were so close to us when one of them had a cold, we caught it."

"I thought your family had money." She said her dad did, not them. "I don't understand the difference. If he had it, wouldn't you have had some as well?"

"No. He was very creative in the way he kept it from us. When Mom passed away he was getting a check each month to care for Allen. Then there was Mom's insurance. He said he had invested it in our futures. So far as I could ever see, all it did was make him a pompous tight ass." She looked at him. "I asked him for a pen set once, to draw. He told me that as my mother's child, I would have to earn the right for them. I never understood that, so I did chores for the neighbors and earned the money for them. He said that I was ungrateful. I told him he was a prick."

He laughed and she smiled at him. It was the first one he'd seen on her since he'd met her. Getting up, he moved to her slowly, wanting more than anything to simply hold her. When she didn't back away, he reached out and touched his finger gently to her cheek.

"You're very beautiful. And I'm so glad that you're in my life." Jack just stared at him and when she licked her lips, he decided that he needed just a taste of her. A small one. "Can I kiss you, love? Will you let me hold you to my body and kiss you?"

"I'm afraid." He nodded but lowered his head to her mouth. "You're going to find out things about me that are going to sicken you. You'll hate me when you do."

"Never." He touched his mouth to her and felt the slick warmth that was all hers. Taking her lower lip into his mouth, he nibbled gently on it as he watched her eyes. They darkened and he could see her desire. Deepening the kiss, he pulled her body to his and wrapped her into his arms as his tongue and hers danced.

Luke wanted her. Not just for sex, even though the thought of taking her to the wall and pounding into her was appealing, but he wanted her in his life. He needed her to be his companion, as stupid as that sounded. He wanted to laugh with her, work with her, and more than anything, he wanted her to love him. Lifting his head from hers, he held her but watched her face as she tried to cover her need.

"Come with me tonight. We need a home of our own. Somewhere I can take you on the kitchen table, feast on you without anyone interrupting us. I want you to have your own studio, a place you can work, play, or even read a book should you want." She nodded and he felt as if he'd been given a gift. "We'll go as soon as I can arrange with the realtor."

"I will pay half." He started to tell her no she wouldn't, that he was the provider, but only nodded. She could pay the entire mortgage if she would stay with him there. Not that it was going to happen, but he would do what she needed. "And if you don't mind, I'd like to have a garden too. Not like your sister's, but something smaller. Way smaller. There are some herbs I'd like to grow that I can use."

"You can cook?" She nodded and told him she did, but didn't get to much because of her apartment being so small. "Okay, then we'll get something with a huge kitchen. Something…shit, I don't know, something you like in that department. Because if you can boil water, you have one up on me."

She laughed and he pulled her tighter to him. He had no idea why the sound of her laughter made him all soft inside, but it did. Pulling her with him, he sat in the chair she'd been in and pulled her into his lap. She didn't fight with him but snuggled up under his chin as she sat there. It was on the tip of his tongue to ask her about the conversation she'd had with Allen, but he decided to wait. Whatever it was, he'd find out soon, he knew it.

It was another hour before Allen stirred. He told them to go away that he was fine, but Jack told him she wanted to stay with him. He told her to go home and leave him to his misery. Finally she said she'd go.

"Jack?" She turned back to Allen just as they were set to go. "Will you do me a favor? Tell them no more drugs. I don't want to get into that again. Please, just tell them something over the counter. This felt really good, but I don't…I don't want to get back there again."

She told him that she would and kissed him on the cheek. Luke felt his wolf stir, but he didn't make too much of a fuss. The sooner he talked to Jack about this the better. But as they were going toward the elevator, he decided that he wouldn't. He wanted her to get all the comfort she could get. Luke groaned when his dad stepped out of the yawning opening and laughed. It was going to be a long night.

~~~

They'd been to three houses. Jack had liked the first one okay, but the second and third were simply ugly. She was pretty sure that the second one had a dead body in the basement, and she told Luke that as they drove to the third one. He told her he'd smelled it as well. His dad said he thought there had been a cat in the place too. Cash said he could smell the cat piss as soon as they got out of the car.

"I've been meaning to ask you." She tensed up and waited for his dad. Jack was so afraid that he'd ask her for something she'd never be able to give him, and she liked the older man enough that she'd get it at all costs. "When you found out you were a wolf, you seemed to take it pretty good. Damned good as a matter of fact. Like you knew about us long before then. Did you? Know about weres, I mean?"

Jack glanced at Luke but he kept his eyes on the road. She wanted to avoid the question, because questions always led to more questions, and she wasn't ready to go into a great many things just yet.

"Do you know a man by the name of Dan Rogers? He said that he'd worked for Luke's brother, Ellis. I know his dad. He...I was hurt one night and he saved me. By becoming a wolf. He always told me that I was just seeing things, but.... A few weeks later, after the incident, I was working late, again, and I pulled up the security video. I watched it seven times before I finally put it away."

"Max is a good man. He brought you something." Luke asked his dad to hand him the box that was lying on the back seat. "I meant to give it to you the other day, but you kept making me forget."

She took the little box and stared at it for several seconds before she opened it. It was her cards, all of them that Allen had sent her. When the second item was handed to her, much bigger than the box, she looked at both men and burst into tears. It was the things she'd wanted from her desk.

"My mom bought me this." She pulled out the little vase that was chipped a long time ago when she'd been moved to another floor at work. She ran her fingers over the lovely little vase. The little angel wasn't expensive, but it meant the world to her. "She said it would watch over me as I worked. It never did...I'm pretty sure she got one that said to turn her back on me, but I love it."

There were other things in the box. Her pens and brushes. Pads of papers that she'd been keeping notes in for herself. There were cheap colored pencils that she'd gotten last month, and her sketch pads she'd had since high school. Jack thumbed through them as they drove to the last house for the night.

"He said that when he heard about your place going up he went there that night and cleaned out your desk. Said that he had to hide it all too. Because he knew that they'd toss it out if it was left for them to care for." Jack nodded at Cash, too overwhelmed to speak yet. "I think he's got something else for you too. Though I've no idea what it could be."

"Your car." She looked at Luke. "He had Dan come for a short visit and they drove it back. Said you'd left it in the street that day and they impounded it. After they talked to the police there, Max was able to get it for you and bring it here. He said that the man was a wolf of good standing and understood what you were going through."

"I don't know what to say." She looked at her things, all the stuff she had of her own in the world, and held them to her breast. Jack started to ask if she could talk to Max, but they were pulling into the drive of the final house before she could. The house…if that's what they called castles this big around here…was magnificent.

"This is lovely." It was also an understatement, but she nodded to Cash. "You think that barn goes with it? Sure would make a nice place to store the tractor if you got yourself one."

"Or a studio." Jack moved up the walkway toward the house as if in a trance as Luke continued talking to his dad. The realtor met them at the door, but she walked by him to go into the house. It was perfect. The entrance hall was something she'd dreamed of her entire life. Running her hands over the chair board, she moved out of the hall into a large open space. And there she fell in love.

The wide staircase nearly filled all the space where she stood. At the top, there was a stain-glassed window that looked to be about ten feet wide and at least five feet high. The stair case split there and moved up onto the landings above her, and she could just make out doors that were all open right now. It looked like five on each side. Luke put his hands on her shoulders and she leaned back into him. He nipped at her ear lobe before speaking softly to her.

"I'm assuming you like this one." She nodded and pulled away to follow the agent. He took them into a sunken living room that had a fireplace in it as big as her entire apartment had been. She wondered if anyone had roasted a beef in it and just caught herself giggling.

The walls were covered in large shelves. Not the kind that would be just for books but for decorations. Fuf-fuf things, she called them. Things that had no value but to the person who sat them on the deep shelves.

The next room they entered was a library. The entire room was surrounded with more shelves. A ladder was stationed on either side of the large windows that looked out over an expansive yard. There was a covered pool there as well as a pool house. And next to it was the barn. She stared at it as she filled the big building with her art supplies in her mind. And a drawing table.

The dining room was across the hallway from the living room. As they entered it, she touched the built in cabinets and the large table. There were enough chairs around it that they could eat at a different place for a week. Eighteen chairs, eight on each side as well as one on each end.

"It stays with the house. The previous owners didn't have room for it in their new houses and they couldn't sell it on an agreeable term for it. So it and the eighteen chairs stay with it if you want them." Luke nodded but she only smiled. To have a family this large to fill this thing would be amazing. She entered the kitchen just as the agent was telling Cash and Luke about the other things that were staying with the house. Jack could not believe that someone would move from this house if they had a kitchen like this.

"You want this one, don't you?" She turned to look at Luke to see if he was making fun of her. All she could see on his face was happiness, but she was still slightly leery of him. "The appliances stay, as well as the large walk in freezer in the back of the pantry. He said there is also two sets of dishes; one is every day, the other is for large family gatherings. The garden you wanted is also back there, but it has been neglected for a very long time."

"Why did they sell it?" He sat on the counter and smiled at her. "They murdered each other and now it can't sell. Not that it matters. You can't afford this. I can't either. Half of whatever they want a month will take everything I have and then some. I wish now we'd gotten the pee house."

"No you don't. And I can afford this house. It's in foreclosure. The couple that lived here divorced and alone, neither of them could afford it. The bank is letting it go for a very reasonable amount." She asked him how much. "Less than whatever amount you have dancing in that pretty head of yours."

The low growl spilled from her lips before she could stop it. Her wolf, the monster inside of her, wanted out. Jack backed away from Luke when he hopped off the counter and came toward her. She shook her head at him and put out her hand.

"I don't know what's going to happen. Don't touch me right now." He ran his finger down her arm, and she moaned. "I don't want this. Make it stop."

"My dad and the agent are gone. I made an offer on the house and they left us." He put his hand over hers and curled his fingers into hers. "Let her go, Jack. Let her out and let me play with her."

"No." But it was too late. Her entire body screamed at her to let go, and she had no power over it any longer. Jack heard clothing ripping and the sound of bones cracking. She wasn't in pain, but she waited for it. When it didn't come, she looked at Luke. He was down on his knees in front of her.

"Christ, you're more beautiful than I thought you'd be." He touched his nose to hers, and she knew that she was no longer human. "You're gray, almost all gray, with a dark streak along your nose and back. Your paws are dark as well—socks we call them—you have four dark socks."

I didn't hurt. He laughed and shook his head. *I thought I'd be in so much pain. She's been fighting me for days now, and I held back because I thought I'd hurt.*

"No, you won't hurt." He stood up and started pulling off his clothes. "We're going to run. You and I are going to run through the fields behind the house. Then I'm going to fuck you hard before we shift and I take you harder as a man."

Jack whimpered and felt her body heat for him. But she did want to run, and as fast as she could. As soon as he opened the back door, she started toward it and fell twice before she could get used to walking on four feet instead of two. The trees seemed to call to her and she took off for the darkest part of the woods.

She could smell everything. Jack felt as if she could hear even the bee's wings as they fluttered in the air. Leaping over fallen logs and brush, she laughed. This was something she'd never equated with being a wolf...the freedom to be out of doors. When she came across a herd of deer, she stilled and watched them. Wishing she could tell them she would rather cut off her arm than to harm them, she knew the exact moment when they saw her. Or smelled her. The big buck made a noise, and they took off like she'd shot them. She was still staring after them when Luke came up beside her.

They must have a den around here. Nodding, she moved forward. She could hear water and wanted to see the stream. *Careful of your paws. You don't want to get caught in a trap. The realtor said that there have been sightings of hunters around here.*

They'd trap on our land? You'll have to put a stop to that. She stopped and turned to him. *Did you really put an offer on this house?*

Yes. And he told me that the bank would take it. They are desperate to get rid of it. And me being the mayor and all, it was a feather in their cap to sell it to me. Apparently your mate is a big deal around here. He moved up beside her and rubbed his body against hers. *I want you. We both do.*

I don't know how this works. He nipped at her shoulder, and she felt her body respond. *Is it always going to be like this between us? Always wanting to have sex no matter where we are?*

I hope so. I love making love with you. Love the way you scream out your release. The way you taste. Everything about you is amazing, and I love you. He moved up behind her and her wolf seemed to understand. She snarled at him, but in the end he mounted her from behind. As soon as he sank his teeth into her shoulder she cried out, but she let him fuck her. It was sort of disappointing until he moved off her and told her to shift.

Her body seemed to ease into being herself again. She was still on her hands and knees and moaned when Luke grabbed her hips. She wanted him to take her, but she needed more than she'd gotten with his wolf.

"I need to come." He growled and nipped at her shoulder with his human teeth. "Luke, I need more. I need to come."

He rolled her to her back and fisted his cock as he stood on his knees over her. She wanted to take him into her mouth, but she wasn't sure he was into that sort of thing. But she wanted him and when she sat up, he laid back on the ground for her.

His cock was thick. She knew that, but it was long too. Wrapping her hands around him, she still had a couple of inches that she couldn't touch. Leaning down to him, she licked his crown and swallowed when he rose up to her mouth.

"That's it, baby. Suck me." She cupped his balls while she licked his length before taking him into her mouth again. Over and over he fucked her this way until she felt his fingers in her hair. Then he pulled her up. "I need to be inside of you when I come. You have to be marked again."

"I do." He growled and pulled her over his hips. Before she could figure out his intentions, she was sliding over his cock and riding him. "Oh yes. This is wonderful."

She rode him slowly, enjoying the way he fit inside of her, the way his groin pressed against her clit with every forward motion. She held him, her fingers on his bare chest just below his nipple. Leaning down, she took one into her mouth and bit down. His hand at the back of her head had her suckling hard at the tiny hard nubbin.

"Come for me." She felt him roll her over and he started pounding deep inside of her. "Come with me, Jack, scream out my name and mark me."

He cupped her ass, bringing her clit to his body every time he slammed into her. When he licked her shoulder, she did the same to him and bit him when she came. Christ, she came so hard darkness seemed to swallow her up.

When she opened her eyes, it could only have been a few seconds, and she looked into his. Luke was looking at her in a way that no man, no one, had ever looked at her before. She could almost bathe herself in his love for her.

Touching his cheek, she knew that Allen was right. He had to know what had happened to her. Had to know…needed to know what she'd been forced to do.

"I'm in love with you." He kissed her gently on the mouth when she spoke. "I'm going to tell you what happened. What really happened the day I left home and never returned. You may hate me afterwards, but I just wanted you to know that I love you."

"Nothing, and I do mean nothing, you could have done will make me love you any less, Jack. I swear to you. Tell me before it eats away at you." She nodded. "Tell me, love. It can't be all that bad."

"I killed a man. I killed him by cutting his throat open, and then I watched him bleed out."

Chapter 8

Mark Wagner moved along the cattle, as he liked to call everyone, as he made his way through the airport. He hated to fly, almost as much as he did anything he had to do, but the kids had been fucking around long enough. They were to come home now and he was going to see that they did. Especially his daughter. She was going to straighten up her act or he'd tell everyone what she'd done.

Mark was flying first class this time out. He could hardly afford it, but he liked the better things in life. He'd always prided himself on that. But the money was nearly gone now, and that was why he was making this ungodly trip out to Ohio, to bring the spawns home so they could support him. After all, they owed him, both of them did. And he was going to make sure they knew it too. Daily.

His wife had been insured, something he'd not expected of her. He'd never given her permission to buy a policy and would have canceled it had he known about it. Now, to think back on it, it would have been a stupid and costly mistake on his part, but he never told anyone that part of the story. He just told whoever asked that she'd provided for him and the family as she did everything. With grace and love.

"Bitch." He looked at the woman who huffed at him. "Well she was. Fucking bitch went and gave me a defective son and a stupid daughter. What the hell was I supposed to do with that? Nobody wanted her after she grew up. It was that mouth of hers. But I taught her a thing or two about that too before she left me."

The woman got up and moved to another seat. Not that Mark cared one wit if she did or not, but he wanted to vent. But as both seats on either side of him were empty, he just thought about what he was going to say to his offspring when he got there. That boy Allen was going to get some help from him too.

Dry. What the fuck did that mean? The last time he'd spoken to his son, before the accident that made the daughter famous, he'd told him that he'd been dry and drug free for nearly six years. Why'd he want to go and do something like that? Mark wondered. So long as he was on the shit, Mark had been getting a tidy sum from the government. It was a burden to care for an addict son. Mark laughed when he thought about how cheap the drugs had been compared to the money he'd gotten from the assistance people.

His zone was called and he moved to get in line to be seated. Mark had a moment of fear that they'd check his carry-on again, but they moved him right on through. He smiled when he thought of how easy it had been to get a gun on a plane, and wondered if the people who ran this place had any idea that it was as simple as going to the right counter and saying the right phrase to get just about anything on that they deemed illegal. Mark was nothing if not connected. And his cane—pretty useless as a cane, as he didn't really need it—hid a nice little stabber when he needed one. Yeppers, Mark thought, he was going to teach them kids of his some nice fine lessons, or they'd know he'd have to kill them. Both the daughter and the defective son.

He shoved his carry-on over the headrest. Mark hated all these rules they had. What he really wanted was to have it in the seat next to him, but the fat broad next to him was smashing herself right up against his part of the seat. What the hell were fat people doing on planes anyway? He leaned his seat back as far as it would go and smiled when the person behind him started cursing. It was fine with him so long as he kept his mouth shut to the stewardess.

As soon as someone tapped him on the shoulder, Mark knew someone had had the balls to say something. The man standing over him surprised him.

"You'll have to put your seat up, sir. At least until we're in the air." He stared at him, a man who had probably dressed in the lavatory of the plane. "Sir? Could you please put your seat up?"

"For what now?" Mark tried to act as if he was slightly feeble minded. It usually got him everything he wanted in the real world. "You want me to do what now?"

"Your seat has to be in an upright position. The plane cannot pull out without everyone in the proper position." Yeah, Mark thought, like his chair and how it was seated was somehow attached to the engine of this thing. "As soon as we're airborne you may lean back. But be mindful of the passengers behind you, please."

"Why do I care what the others are doing?" He let it slip out before he could think it was the wrong thing to say. "What are you talking about, young man? My seat is up."

The man actually reached over and flipped his seat up. Mark was so shocked by the move that he was still sitting there when the little bastard moved away. The nerve of the prick. He started to put his hand on the lever to put his seat back when a voice behind him spoke. It was so close to his ear that Mark actually flinched from it.

"You put that seat back again and I will make sure your trip is made from a prone position. As in wrapped up in a body bag." Mark started to turn but a sharp pinch to his neck made him still. "You think real hard on that, Mr. Wagner. If you so much as act like you're going to give anyone around you a hard time, I will make it my business to fuck you up. Gun or no gun."

Mark sat very still. He didn't so much as reach for his belt to loosen it when the sign came on that it was possible. The woman next to him no longer concerned him because his entire focus was on the man, the threat behind him.

The flight, mostly in a blur, was over before he finally got up the nerve to look behind him. He got up to get his things from the overhead and snuck a glance. There was only a woman there, and a child. A small one too. He looked further back in the seats and the only man he could see was one nearly to the back, well behind the curtain that divided first class, his area, from the rest of the plane. The only other man in the section he was in was a man in his later years, and he was sleeping soundly. Mark had to sit down again to get his breathing under control.

Where had he come from? Where was he now? The first class seating was wide, the seats far apart. How had he even been smashing the man at all? Mark started to ask the flight attendant about him, but he was busy helping the others off. It wasn't until the fat broad asked him if he was planning to leave that he got up. Mark was standing in the lobby of the smallish airport when he realized he must have been sleeping.

No you weren't. He looked around. *You're not going to find me, you ass wipe. I've a taste of you now so you'll forever be in my mind. And me in yours.*

"What the hell do you mean? Where are you? Show yourself, you coward." People in the lobby stared at him and he flushed. "Where are you?"

I'm a friend of your daughter's friend. I'm...let's just say I'm going to be guiding you through this visit of yours, and if I see anything or hear anything that pisses me off, I'm going to come after your ass. And trust me, you do not want me to be pissed. The laughter again had him cringe. *You'll want to ask Dan when you see him if the name Steward means anything to him.*

"Dan? I don't know a Dan. I'm here to bring my children to heel." He tried to lower his voice as others were beginning to stare at him openly now. "I'm not going to be visiting anyone while here. Where are you? I've asked you that several times now."

I'm nearer than you think, and further away than I'd like to be. Mark waited for him to say more but nothing was forthcoming. As he made his way to the luggage terminal, he heard the man again. This time it had Mark scrambling for his carry-on. *I've taken the liberty of removing your gun from the bag you have. A man like you, a man on parole, shouldn't have one anyway. I'll give it to another friend of mine when I see him. Have a lovely visit, Mark Wagner.*

Mark watched his luggage, a small bag, roll around twice before he got up to retrieve it. He'd been had was all he could think of what had just happened. Someone had found out he was here and now they were fucking with him. Mark moved out into the fresh air and looked around for a taxi, anything that would convey him to the hotel. It took him nearly thirty minutes to realize that not only wasn't anyone going to carry him away from here, but he was going to have to have someone call his children to have them come for him. It was not the way he wanted this trip to begin.

"Come to the airport and get me. I'll be just inside the place. Don't be long." He hated to leave a message, but Allen would no longer take his calls. When he tried to call his daughter, all he got from her was that the number had been disconnected. What the hell? Was she out of money too?

Nearly four hours later someone came into the lobby and shouted his name. The man…well, there was no way he was going to ride anywhere with this person. His pants were dirty, his ball cap looked as if he'd rolled it in manure, and he had enough paint on his pants that he looked like that famous painter had used him as a model. He was simply a mess. Then the man looked at him and started coming at him. Mark stood up.

"It might have saved me some time had you answered me." He picked up his bag and Mark started to protest. "I'm Dan Rogers. I work with your daughter's mate, Luke Emerson. I was sent to get you."

"Dan?" Mark felt his face pale, and he had to grab onto the chair next to him. "You know a man by the name of Steward?"

The grin told it all. He knew him. And Mark had a feeling that this Steward person had talked to Dan and was the reason he was here to get him, to make him suffer more. When Mark took a step back, Dan put down the case and crossed his arms over his massive chest.

"Are we going to have a problem?" Mark shook his head. "Then let's get going. I'm not going to hurt you. Yet, at any rate. Besides, I think you're going to be surprised at how well your kids can take you on now. If I were you, I'd think long and hard about fucking with them. Especially your daughter. Jack has…changed."

"They most certainly will not do a thing to me. I'm their father. I'm here to bring them in line, not listen to them whine about what they want." Dan only nodded and walked away. Mark had to carry both his pieces of luggage or be left behind. He was going to take care of this as soon as they were settled in whatever contraption he came to pick him up in.

The truck had a name blazing across the door that looked impressive. He started to comment on it, the nice way that the crew seemed to be working hard; the truck, with the same name on it, looked clean, professionally done. As he was told to dump his things in the back, Mark stood back and looked at the drawing harder. Whoever did this needed to work for him. As a man of all kinds of trades, this would be a feather in his cap.

"She did it." Mark looked at Dan. "Your daughter did it. Jack. She sat down and drew it out in less time than it took Ellis, my boss, to tell her what he wanted. Looks good, doesn't it?"

"She has no talent to speak of." Mark was soured on the drawing now. So much so that he wanted to point out the flaws in it, but really, he couldn't see any. Just as the big truck started and was moving into traffic, he realized that the man was laughing.

"Perhaps you can tell me what you find so funny? Is it that I knew better than the drawing to be my daughters? I assure you, I know her much better than most. She will lead you down a merry path and then leave you out to die if you should let her." Dan glanced at him and frowned. "You'll see if I'm correct or not. My daughter is quite the schemer when it suits her."

"Jack Wagner? Tall, dark hair, blue eyes, right?" Mark nodded. He honestly had no idea what color the daughter's eyes were, as he'd never really cared to get close enough to her to look. "Yeah, you're all wrong about that woman. Christ, she has Luke all tied up in knots and they haven't even said their 'I do's' yet."

"My daughter is not marrying anyone." Dan laughed. "I'll put an end to that the minute I see this young man. There is no way he'll take her on once he finds out what sort of person she is. Did she tell you that she murdered a man?"

"Nope. But knowing her, she had a good reason." Mark looked out the window. There was no talking to some people. The rest of the ride was made in silence, other than telling him which hotel he was staying in. As he was dropped off, literally at the door, Mark had a feeling that he was going to be seeing more of that man.

As he moved into the lobby of the hotel, he noticed all the work going on. Most of the construction was happening behind the desk. Mark was annoyed that he had to put up with this sort of thing.

After he was taken to his room, his bags put on the bed and the boy dismissed without a tip, he tried to call Allen again. There was no reason for this and he was going to make sure his son knew how displeased he was about his treatment. Mark lay down on his bed and tried to get his nerves under control. It wasn't so much his nerves as it was his anger. His children were completely out of control. It was a good thing he was there to bring them back in line.

~~~

"Took him there myself. He's a turd if you ask me." Luke tried to think how the hell he was going to tell Jack her dad was in town without upsetting her when Dan smiled at him. "She can take him. He's a prick and a bastard, but she's a good deal stronger than she was when she ran away from home."

"But he's still her dad." Dan nodded and sipped his tea. They were having tea and sandwiches before going back to work on the dining room. He had hoped to get it finished before now, but there were issues they were running into. Like the fact that the police had been out here five times checking permits.

"That prick has to go too." Luke nodded and wondered if Dan had a plan to get rid of the chief of police. "No plan, just stating some truth. I have all the paperwork we need and we both know it. And for that matter, if he comes out here again, I think Jack just might tear him a new ass."

"She was pretty pissed last time." In fact, she'd run him to his vehicle when he'd told her to back the fuck up from him. Jack was taking her wolf to heart and letting her run the show whenever she needed it. Not that she shifted, but she did let her go just enough to let Granger know that she'd meant business. Just as he was going to get them something else to eat, Jack came into the kitchen, and whatever had happened, it wasn't going to go well for the other person.

"My father is here." Luke nodded. "You knew he was here and didn't tell me. Thanks a whole fucking lot. What if he'd come here? I would have been unprepared to get away."

"You don't have to be afraid of him. But I only just found out too. Someone that we know saw him get onto a plane and notified us only after he landed. Dan picked him up at the airport and took him to a hotel. He seems to think you and Allen are going back with him." Her snort made him laugh. "You're the big bad wolf that scares police to wet themselves. Your father is going to be a piece of cake. And Allen is still being watched at the hospital. I have two men on him at all times."

"I'm going to see him today." Luke knew that, he'd made arrangements for her to have a driver too. "And then I'm going to go and see Max. He's got my car keys and more stuff he wanted to give me."

He wanted to tell her to let him take care of it. Needed for her to allow him to handle everything for her, but she would never grow, never feel good about this if he did that. Plus, he was pretty sure she'd kick his ass if he tried. And since Luke was the mayor-elect, having his mate kick his ass would not go over well.

"I want you to not see your sire alone. I'm not telling you that you can't, just that I don't want you to. He's dangerous. When he was ready to board, he had a gun. A friend of ours took it from him when he wasn't aware." Luke would have to tell her about Steward too. He was just waiting for the right moment to let her know that not only were there vampires in the world, but one was his good friend. Steward Thomas was a bit...he was a lot strange and an old vampire. "Your sire means you both ill will, and I don't want you to get hurt when he tries to take you."

"Sire? You called him that twice. Is it because you don't think of him as my dad? Neither do I. And I like that. But he has a cane. You have to watch out for that too. He doesn't think we know, but it's a sword...sort of. He calls it his pick. And I guess that's basically what it is. A long shaft of silver that he has sharpened to a point." Luke wondered what else that man had brought with him when Jack continued. "It's what he used a few times on men who didn't deal well with him. Me too once, and I have no idea how many times on Allen. Enough, I suppose, to make him afraid. What kind of person makes their children afraid of them? I never would."

Luke was looking forward to meeting Mark Wagner. The man was a real piece of work and he for one wanted to see him fail. And he was going to. There was no way in hell that either Allen or Jack was going back with him. Not while he was still breathing. And he sure as shit wasn't going to hurt them again.

"I have him under surveillance. There are about two dozen wolves in the lobby of the hotel under the guise of working. They are working, but not only at their job." She nodded and he could feel her tension. Instead of commenting on it, he turned to Dan. "Where is your dad staying? With you?"

"Yeah. He's driving me nuts too. Not in a bad way, but he wants to work with me. I asked Ellis and he said to give him a job if he really wants it. I don't guess he's going back to Anderson/Shelling." He felt Jack tense up. "They are having some problems there, and he said they're not long for being in business."

"They have a lot of good clients there." Jack got up to pace. "I worked with a lot of them. Personally too. There is some major money to be had if they have to go elsewhere. I wonder what happened."

"You." They both looked at Max when he walked in the house. "Hello, darling. I've missed you something…holy shit balls, you've gone and got yourself a mate."

"I have." Jack flushed brightly and looked at him. "This is Luke Emerson. He's the one that says I'm his mate."

"You are his, honey." Luke felt his wolf shift under his skin; not like he wanted to murder the older man, but more like he was finding a friend. He'd never met Max before, but had liked what he'd heard about him. And the fact that he'd saved all of Jack's things when they were being tossed out made him like him all the better. "I was telling Dan here that the place hasn't been the same since you left. That client you had? What was his name? He had the dog food. Said to Anderson if you aren't there any longer, then he was going elsewhere. You should call him up and offer to take him on yourself."

Luke watched her face. He could tell she wanted to, but only shook her head. As they moved into the other part of the house talking about the man and his company, he looked at Dan. The smile on his face said volumes.

"You can do her up right if I get her to do this, can't you?" Dan smiled bigger and nodded. "I have to talk to Hunter, but I think he'd go for it. That building in the Walker district would be perfect for her."

"Nope. The one across from the courthouse would be better. Lots of light, three levels of work area. And there's enough old crap in it to make her a start on the furniture.

It used to be a copier firm about ten years ago." Dan stood up. "If you get the okay from Hunter, we can start in a few days. Men are begging to work for us now that Emerson is on the company logo."

"I'm sure they know you are there as well." Dan only shrugged. "Ellis is a good man. He'll help you a great deal with getting you on the road to having your own company back. Bigger and better."

"I know that. Hell, I'm planning on him helping me with it. Talked to Slone and Hunter about some of the things he's doing now. I like him and I'm proud to be a part of his company." Dan laughed. "For now. Soon, after I get all I can from him, I'm going to run him out of business."

As he left the house, Luke contacted Hunter. He set up a meeting for the next morning at his office and went to find his mate. He was just coming into the living room when he heard her tell Max that she'd love to do business as an advertising firm, but she'd never make it with the little money she had. Luke decided to sit her down and have a long conversation about their money. And then take her up to their bedroom and ravage her again. Having a mate was a wonderful thing.

Chapter 9

Hank saw the men wandering around the building when he went to work the next day. He glanced at his watch and saw that it was just after noon, so he wondered how long they'd been there before now. Calling his second in command, the man said he'd not been out since he'd come in that morning.

"I know that you don't own it if that helps you." Hank asked him who did. "That Emerson bitch. She bought it about ten years ago when Copious Copies went under. Kinda of liked that place too. They had the best prices on making picture copies."

And they had been a front to one of his business, too. Along with Conklin, Hank would run stolen items out the back while the owner, a man who had been as stupid as they came, would take a cut off the top. Usually about one percent. And one percent of millions was a good deal of money. But his wifey had caught him with his pants down and his dick buried deep in some customer one day, and they all lost their extra money. She took him for all of it and then some. Last Hank heard he'd died and she was still living off the money.

"You get a couple of men together and find out what they think they're doing. I don't remember seeing no permits hanging there when I walked by there last night." Sam said he'd get right on it. "And call up Osborne and tell him what's going on. I'm thinking the city has a contract with Osborne in that they do all the city limit shit that needs done."

If there wasn't a contract, he'd have one made up that said just what he wanted it to. Them fucking dogs were not going to get anything so far as he was concerned. He was just going into his office when he saw her. The fucking Emerson bitch. She stood up when he started to walk by her.

"You can't avoid me forever, Chief." He turned so quickly to tell her off that he spilled his coffee all down the front of him. Her laughter did nothing to improve his already testy mood.

"I'm the chief of police, not some two bit sheriff, Emerson. You'd do well to remember that." She laughed again and he wanted to slap it off her face. Instead he went into his office and started to slam the door in her face when the fucking mayor stood up. The fucker was at his desk, and he looked like he was measuring it up for someone else. Before he could tell him to get the hell out, Bitch walked in.

"We have an appointment. An hour ago, but we have one." She sat down in the only other chair, and Hank glared at the mayor. "He's going to help me explain to you, yet again, the rules this seat has to abide by in order for me to continue to help the city with all the needs they have. As of right now, you and your men are in direct violation of about a dozen laws. Then there are the ones that are laws that you are simply breaking. Like the deplorable cells that are — "

"You think I should give them silk sheets and room service? Hell, woman, I don't even have that and I'm chief of police." He thought she said something like "for now" but he didn't want to ask her to repeat it. "I'm doing what needs to be done to keep law and order in this town. You already crossed the line when you got Conklin arrested. What do you think is going to happen when there is no police here either?"

"Order? The laws enforced? Perhaps we could expect someone to come to work on time. Or even to work a forty hour work week. When was the last time you bothered to be to work during working hours?" He snarled at her and she laughed. "You don't frighten me, Chief. I have meals that give me more fight than you will when I tangle with you."

"These are the things we'd like for you to take care of." The file was in his hand before he could tell the mayor to fuck off. "In there you will also find a list of violations that need to be taken care of right now, as well as a few things that need to be addressed about the condition of the cells. I know firsthand that the mattresses are a bit on the lumpy side and the pillows need to be replaced."

"Maybe I can put you back down there and you can tell me what you think about that." Mayor Emerson only smiled as they stood up. "You better watch yourself there, dog. We don't like your kind around here."

Hank nearly fell back when the man went from wearing a suit to being completely covered in fur. When he growled at him, standing among his shredded clothing, Hank had a moment where he wondered if he was going to piss himself again. The last time, the bitch had made him when she'd come after him. But this dog looked a good deal meaner than she'd been. And a lot bigger. Hank took a step back and tried to reason with him.

"Nice doggie." The animal snapped very close to his dick, and the bitch laughed. "What the fuck is wrong with you? Tell him to back the fuck off before I shoot him."

"I wouldn't do that if I were you. He'll have your hand off your wrist before you can get the thing cleared of your holster. And stop calling him a dog. He's a wolf. A big werewolf. And he's not very happy with you." Hank wasn't too thrilled himself but refrained from saying so. "Sit down and shut up."

Hank did as she commanded but kept his eye on the dog...wolf. He glanced at her once when she sat down, but otherwise watched the teeth that seemed to grow longer and sharper as the mayor watched him. Hank was pretty sure they weren't growing, but with this fucking family, who knew what they could do?

"Now what?" She giggled, and he looked at her. "You think this is fucking funny? You come into my office, make me stand when he sits at my desk, and one of you fucking changes into a dog...err, wolf. And now you sit there laughing. This is so going to cost you. When this meeting or whatever the hell you call it is over, I'm going to have every one of my officers hunt you down every time you come out of that fucking mansion of yours. See if I don't."

"You do not frighten me, Granger. Few men do, but you are not one of them. And as for your threats, they mean shit right now. In four days an investigator is coming in and going over your books. They were kind enough to start on them several days ago, but now...well, now it seems they have a bunch of questions. Mostly about—"

"You can't have someone come in here. I demand that you call this off." She only looked at him with a cocked brow. Hank stood up, and the wolf growled again. "Call them off. I mean it. They're not going to find shit, and I don't want them here. This is not going to happen in my town."

"Your town? I guess you have a reason to think that, but it's not. And I'm sure you don't want them here. However, they are coming and, well, I guess we'll find out. And what do you have to worry about if, as you have so eloquently put it, they aren't going to find shit?" She leaned back in the chair and stared at him. Hank felt fear tangle with his anger and he tried his best to control it. He knew that if he made even a small movement toward her, he'd be dead. And for some reason, he had his doubts it would be by the wolf. The woman looked like she could have chewed him up and spit him out without even thinking too much about it.

"Let's start over. I think we've gotten off on the wrong foot." He leaned back and tried to look as relaxed as she seemed to be. "You say they're coming here. Okay, for what purpose? To get rid of me. That's not going to happen and we both know that. I'm an elected official and we both know that so long as the people want me here…well, darling, I'm here to stay."

"They're looking at the voter registration as well." His entire body froze up. Blood seemed to stop pumping to his extremities, and his heart felt like it no longer beat. He tried to think over the loud buzzing in his ears, but her words, so softly spoken, were what was going to ruin him, and give him a very long, very hard prison sentence. "I can see by your face that you're thinking this isn't going to go well. Did you know that my name, as well as several hundred others, are on that list as voting for you? I'm reasonably sure that I didn't vote for you. A few of the names also turned out to be dead men. How do you suppose that happened?"

"I don't know what you're talking about." But he did. Voter fraud was a huge thing to the state and bigger to the country. He was fucked if they even knew half the names on the list. There was a stiff penalty for each and every name he'd used. "I'm not sure I want to continue this meeting without a lawyer."

She stood up after nodding to him. The wolf stood there for several seconds more before he turned and looked at the bitch. When she smiled, Hank felt the hair on his neck dance.

"He said to tell you that for each case of fraud the penalty is two grand as well as five years in prison. For each one. I'm pretty sure you're going to be very old if not long dead before you can get out." She turned her back on him and Hank wanted to get up and tear her throat out. But the wolf stared at him. As soon as she left the wolf moved toward him and sniffed his leg. Then the fucking bastard turned and pissed on him. Hank was too stunned to react, and it wasn't until after the dog left him standing there with wet shoes and stained pants that every curse word he knew and some he made up came vomiting from his mouth. Hank was going to kill these people if it was the last thing he did.

~~~

"Hello? Is this Jack Emerson?" Jack tried to recognize the voice, but all she could think of was being called Emerson. "I was given this number by Luke."

"This is Jack." She didn't confirm the Emerson part, but she was going to talk to Luke about it. "I'm not sure who this is. I'm sorry."

"Course you don't. When we worked together I never met you. There was always...never mind that. I'm Kyle Sweet. I have the Sweet Puppy Company." She sat up straighter in her chair and looked at Audra Bates, the new cook, when she handed her a pad of paper. "I was wondering if you and I can sit down and have a little pow-wow? I have heard that you're setting up shop on your own and I want to get in on the ground floor. And I got a feeling that as soon as it's out there, you're going to have to run clients off with a shotgun. Damn, I'm glad I found you."

"Ground floor?" He laughed, and Jack flushed. "I'm not really sure what you mean, Mr. Sweet. I thought you were working with Anderson/Shelling. I used to work for them, but I've been...well, dismissed."

"I heard about that. Sure, we all did. How you were taking on more than you could chew up. I even heard one rumor that you were dead. Not any more true than you being carried by that company for a lot of years. He tried to tell me that they'd been...well, they'd been working to figure out how to let you go for years. Moron. What does he take me for, a fool? I'm not, let me tell you that." He laughed this time and it sounded slightly bitter. "Me and a few of their clients have left them. Breach of contract and all. Did you know that in a meeting with them just last week they had the nerve to tell me that I'd have to wait on my new product advertising? Said it was due to them downsizing. Downsizing my ass. They're losing clients like it's a house fire and every man for themselves."

"But what does this have to do with me?" She looked up when Luke sat down beside her. He was dressed for work, and she thought about mussing him again. As soon as the thought popped into her head, he leaned in and nibbled at her neck. She was sure that Mr. Sweet heard her when she moaned. Luke could do things to her that had her doubting she wasn't a sexual deviant.

"I want to hire you. Be one of your first customers. I got me a feeling you won't be downsizing anytime soon, nor will you put more on your plate than you can handle." She told him she would never do that. "Good. I'll be in your little town tomorrow. I have reservations at the hotel there in town, and that nice husband of yours is making sure that everything is set up on my end too. Been talking to a man…what was his name? Wagner, Allen. Nice man. Gonna try and steal him away when I'm there too."

"Tomorrow?" She was having a hard time concentrating and reached out to grab Luke by the balls. When he rocked into her hands, she tightened her grip on him and he stopped. "Tomorrow you'll be in town?"

"Good, good. I'll see you then." He hung up before she could ask him for what. As Luke moved back from her, his balls protected by his hand now, Jack glared at him.

"There are a number of things I'd like to discuss with you." He grinned. "And if you think that charming grin will get you laid, you're fucking nuts. Why is Kyle Sweet coming to see me tomorrow to get in on the ground floor of my business when I have no idea what he's talking about? And why am I Jack Emerson? I don't remember anyone asking me or me saying yes to marrying you. And so you know, now would not be a good time to ask."

"I meant to talk to you about it last night, but you got me off track." He ran his hand up her knee to her thigh. "If you want to go up and get me off again, I'll be more than glad to let you."

"Behave." She looked at Audra, who laughed and left them alone. "What is she going to think? I'm betting right now she's thinking she's made a horrible mistake coming here. And damn it, I like her sweet rolls. And don't try to change the subject. What did he mean?"

"We have a building downtown. In fact, we have several. I bought two off of Slone just last month, and the other I got in a public auction. Contents included. I've had Dan go in and look it over, and he said it would be perfect for you." Her first thoughts were he was moving her out of his house, but he continued before she could ask him what she'd done. "There is plenty of light for you, all natural, and he said that adding more work stations as well as lighting would be no problem. Also there is adequate parking in the rear for your employees. As well as enough rooms for you to—"

"Wait." He stopped talking and grinned again. "Employees? I have no clue what you're talking about. I don't have anyone...." Then it hit her. Mr. Sweet, the building, as well as workstations all fell into place. Her breathing hurt, her head spun, and before she could do much more than try to learn to breathe again, her head was between her legs and she was staring at his feet.

"Damn it all to hell. I knew you'd take it badly but not like this. I thought I'd get it all fixed up and present it to you. Even had Allen make a list...are you all right?" She struggled and he let her up, but he didn't sit down again. "I wanted to surprise you. I thought...I hoped it would be something you'd love. Your own company."

"I can't do this." He nodded and sat down beside her again. "I don't know the first thing about advertising. Well, I do, but not how to run a business. I'm just an okay artist. I have a talent for putting a pretty thing on paper with some words. Nothing more."

"That's sounds a great deal like an advertising firm." He took her hand into his when she slapped his shoulder. "Slone said she'd help you get started. Jarrett told me that he'd come in and set you up to get your computers going. Graham and Ellis are going to help with getting everything set up the way you want, and Lee said he'd cook you food when you worked late. Hunter said that he had a few men and woman that would love to come in and do grunt work for you."

"I don't have money." He told her they did. "I can't use your money for a business that will more than likely fail in the first week. I just can't do that."

"Jack, you have to do this. And you have a client already. Sweet has called me several times to talk to you. I had no idea until you said so that he'd gotten our home number. But he is already willing to work with you and you've not even opened your doors." He kissed her hand then turned it over and licked her palm. "And as for the Emerson name, that too was going to be something we talked about. I want you to marry me."

The ring felt heavy in her palm. She stared at it for several seconds before he picked it up again and got down on his knee in front of her. As he slipped it up over her knuckle she watched his face, wondering if this was a cruel joke.

"I love you. And I think that I always have. No, that's not right. My heart has been ready for you my entire life. Just waiting for you to come along and fill in the place.

You are the best thing that has ever happened to me, and will forever be the most wondrous thing in the universe to me. I want to have children with you, watch you grow large with them. I can't wait to see you have our child suckle at your breast, hold them to you in love. I need you in my life and want you to be my wife." The ring slid over her finger to settle like it had been there her entire life on her ring finger. She looked up at him and he told her again he loved her. "Will you marry me?"

"I'm afraid." He nodded. "I've never loved anyone before. Never even…there are so many things that you might find out you hate me for later. And if I say yes, it means forever."

"To me as well." She watched him as he waited, knowing that he did truly love her and her him, but would it be enough? As soon as she nodded, telling him yes, he stood up and pulled her into his arms. The kiss, a hungry consuming kiss, sealed the deal.

"I wish I didn't have to go in." She felt his cock as he rocked into her. "Christ, I want to lay you over this table and eat you. Then fuck you until you scream out my name."

"Please." He laughed and pulled back. "You're not playing very fair. Getting me all wet and then leaving me hanging."

His low growl made her laugh, and he moved back more when she reached for him. It occurred to her that she had a great deal of power over him, and wanted to see how far it would go. Just as she reached for him again, his cell phone rang. And she could tell by the tone it was Allen. Play would have to wait.

"I'm leaving now. Are they there?" Allen must have said no. "Good. Is everything set up? The tables and conference rooms ready?"

Luke pulled her to him for a quick and thorough kiss before turning and leaving her wanting. As soon as the door closed behind him, Audra came in and handed her the handset of the house phone. She nearly missed what the caller was saying, her mind was so fuzzy.

"I expect you to be here at noon and not a moment later." She realized then it was her sire, the man she had been dreading talking to for days now. "And you're going to get the notion out of your head right now that you can talk to me in a manner that you did when you left me. I will have you respect me, or so help me I'll let that family know just what sort of person you really are."

It was on the tip of her tongue to tell him that Luke knew. As did Hunter. When she'd told Luke that she'd killed a man, Hunter had been called in as well. She was still learning all the ins and outs of being in a pack, but Hunter told her she was going to be just fine. She hoped so.

"I can't be there at noon. You'll just have to change the time to a better one to suit me." Which wasn't true, but she wasn't going to let him run over her. Not yet at any rate. But he was her father and he had a way about him that made her obey. "I can come there at one and I'll be with someone. So either work with me or not, I don't care."

"You will not be with someone. This is a family meeting and you and I and that brother of yours will settle this thing up before we leave here. I've already stayed longer than I want. You'll come alone." She didn't say anything. "Did you hear me, Daughter? I said you'll be here at noon alone and you'll not make me wait."

She was nodding, her body doing what her mind was telling her not to do. But before she voiced her accession, she stiffened up and took a deep breath. It was high time she realized she was an adult and not his child.

"We'll be there at one." She hung up the phone and tried to think what she should do now. Going alone wasn't something she really wanted to do, but she had no one she could ask. When the phone rang again, she squeaked at it before Audra picked it up, answering it for her.

"It's Mrs. Emerson. She asked if you were busy." When she shook her head, the phone was suddenly in her hand. Before she spoke, however, Audra took her chin in her hand and spoke low. "You're a wolf. A she-wolf. A strong animal that hunts prey and kills what pisses it off. This man, your sire, is nothing to you unless you let him. Are you going to let him? Are you going to let him rule a life that he's no part of?"

"He will hurt me." She snorted. "I don't want to leave here. I want...I want my own life. With all of you."

Audra told her to talk to the alpha, the she-alpha on the phone. As soon as she took the phone off mute, she asked Slone if she'd have lunch with her father and her today.

"It won't be pleasant. It might even be loud, but I have to meet him and I'm afraid I'm not strong enough to do it on my own." Slone laughed and Jack wanted to cry. "I'm sorry. Why on earth would you want to have lunch with an idiot and a fool?" She started to hang up.

"I guess those are two words that I'd use to describe your father. But not you. Never you. And I'd love to have lunch with the two of you. Provided you let me record it if things get nasty. I will have to show Hunter and he will love it too. I was laughing because of what you said. You're more than strong enough to take him on. Hell, I think you were even without your wolf. And yes, I'd love to. But you and I are going to see that building of yours first. I might need you for a few things, and I am going to be the first customer, not the dog food guy."

"He wants to get in on the ground floor." She looked at her ring as the light sparkled around the room. "I don't know a thing about running a business. I'm not even sure what to call myself."

"I was thinking on that too. Not a lot, mind you, but between throwing up this morning. I think you should call it something simple, something elegant that suits you. And a logo. A sharp drawing that shows you at your best."

Jack picked up the pencil and started making notes, and drew a few pictures as they set up the time to meet. She was still drawing on the pad when Audra told her that she had another call.

"Howdy, girl. I heard tell through the wolf circle that you're opening your own little shop." She laughed when Max did. "You need yourself a nice little janitor? I find myself in need of a job, and my missus can't stand me around the house we're renting much longer. We have a bead on a house but nothing yet."

"I'd love that. But I don't know where to find you those sandwiches here. Do you?" He told her about the diner and that they had the best ones in the country. "Then it's a deal. But you have to tell your wife that as part of your hiring package, you get a meal a day. All right?"

"Hell yeah, it's all right." She heard him shouting to someone, who must have been his wife. "She said to tell you thanks. I think she was ready to murder me and you saved my life."

She talked to him for a few more minutes as she played with the note pad. Jack missed having her things around her all the time, and made a mental note to ask Luke if she could set up a room in their new house. She looked up when Audra cleared her throat.

"Time to get going, miss. It's going on ten now." Jack looked at the clock then at the pad of paper. "You do fine work there. My son, he loves to draw too. Says it's relaxing. I think it works, because since he got out of school for the break, he sleeps later and later."

Her voice said she was worried about her son. Jack had no idea why, but she found herself wanting to help them both. So before she left the big kitchen she told Audra to have her son Josh come by and talk to her. Maybe she could get him some work at her firm. Jack was moving up the stairs to get ready for her trip when it occurred to her that she was a business owner.

"Mother fuck." She sat on the steps with her head between her legs again as what had just happened seemed to wash over her. Then she got up and went to their room. She was Jack Emerson and she was a business owner and had people wanting her work. Her father was going to learn to live with her not bowing down before him, and the sooner the better.

Chapter 10

Luke handed over every file he could find. There had been a moment there when they despaired of finding anything but empty boxes in the big storage room in the basement, but Allen had remembered that payments were being made monthly to a storage rental firm and he got them the information. It had not just been packed with boxes of files, but they also found a large stash of weapons and ammo. The Feds took an immediate interest in those as well.

"We got a call today. From the chief of police." The man, Bart Towers, didn't look up from the mess in front of him as he spoke. "Said that we were to look out for you. Seemed to think that you and that young man that works for you are trying to frame him. I guess he got wind that we were looking into his businesses. I'm glad. I love it when they squirm around on a hook like that."

"And did he tell you how I was going about this?" Towers just laughed. "I assure you, sir, that everything is on the up and up here. I'm working through a great mess I was left by my predecessor."

"Conklin." Luke nodded. "Yeah, I'm working on that one too. Seems that man has a great deal to say regarding the chief as well. And there's not a lot of it nice. Mostly darn right nasty if you ask me. He has rolled over on a few men as a matter of fact. Do you know Osborne and his construction company?"

"I do. We're looking into them as well here on a more local level. There have been some contracts handed out that we can't seem to find any bids for." Towers nodded. "You know about that as well?"

"We do. And I'd ask you not to look much more than you already have. We have...let's just say we have someone on it now. She'll contact you in a few days." Towers looked up at him then. "Your father, Cash, he and I go way back. Did he tell you about me?"

"No." Luke wanted to ask his dad now but knew that he was working on the tractor this morning. And he was afraid to distract him. His dad had volunteered to mow their back yard and was having the time of his life when he'd left this morning. "My dad is a good man."

"He is. The best. And when you talk to him, tell him that I'm still married to her and that he's to stay away." Luke laughed. His father had a way with women. He'd never strayed when his mom was alive, but he flirted a great deal. Luke remembered his mom never saying anything, but being very tolerant of him. He supposed his father needed to flirt like people had to breathe, and she saw that in him.

"I'll do that." Towers nodded and looked back at the files. Luke had a feeling the man wanted to say more but was working up to it. Deciding that he'd find him when he was ready to talk, he moved to his office. Luke was just sitting down when Allen came into the room.

He'd only been back to work for a half day yesterday. He was still badly bruised up and he used a cane to walk.

When Luke told him to rest, he told him that he needed to work, to show the men who had hurt him that he wasn't going to let them take this from him. As soon as he sat down, Allen smiled.

"My father is in town." Luke nodded. He'd meant to tell him before but forgot. "He's demanded a meeting with me...and Jack, but she is going to meet him today. I'm supposed to tell you that she's got company and that Slone...Mrs. Emerson...is recording it for us."

"She'll be fine." Allen nodded and handed him some slips of paper. "There are nine calls from a man by the name of Pierce Grover. He's trying to contact Jack. I didn't tell him anything. Also, Granger called but I blew him off. He wants a meeting with you as man to man he said."

"He's going to make my wolf pissy if he keeps this up." He looked over the phone calls and laid them on the desk. "She found out this morning. Sweet called her just like you said he would."

"I figured he wouldn't be put off much longer. And neither will Grover. Those men really want her to work with them." Luke nodded. "I have the list from Max too. He said that as a man who does clean up, no one noticed him taking out her desk things. I'm glad he gave her list of clients to you as well."

"She's going to need the boost. When I left her this morning she was having doubts. I called in the troops." Allen asked who. "Slone."

"She frightens me just a little. I have no idea why but whenever I'm around her, I want to drop to the ground and bury my face in the dirt." Luke laughed. "She's a wonderful woman, but scares me all the same."

"Oh, before I forget, Slone has a place for you. It's not huge, but it's nice. Dan and Ellis are working on it now.

The roof needed to be repaired and carpet replaced, so you'll be able to move in soon." Allen looked away. "I told you I would find you someplace safe. And this is on pack land so you'll have wolves, both wild and like me, all over the place."

"I don't know how to…I have very little money. I'm making payments to some of my older bills that I incurred when I was younger." Luke knew about those and some other things that Allen was working to take care of. Like the car loan that he no longer had the car for, the restitution he was making to someone he'd hurt while he'd been high, and the money he was paying out of his own pocket to have his mom's grave cared for. Jack was doing the same thing, though her money was for the funeral costs.

"You should know now that if you make a single threat of a payment to her she will have your face-planted in the dirt forever. Slone is doing this because she feels she owes you. And if you tell her no, she will hurt you." Allen nodded and looked away. He was the most tenderhearted man he knew.

"My sister…did she tell you what Father has over her?" Luke nodded. "He'll tear her down with it. Hurt her in ways that will be hard to see. She never meant to…Father forced her hand."

"She told me." Allen stood up and so did Luke. "I'm going to take care of her. And you if you'll let me. I owe you more than I can ever repay you."

"Don't hurt her. And don't let her be hurt. It's all the payment I'll ever need." Allen left his office and shut the door behind him. Luke sat there for several minutes before he got to work. He'd never hurt either of them. But he was touched that Allen had so much confidence in the fact that Luke would protect her.

As noon came and went Luke worked on getting the budget ready for the monthly meeting. He found a few things on it that he needed to look into and made notes. As he was finishing up the budget he saw a file on his desk marked Library Project in Slone's neat handwriting. Opening it, he looked at the proposal and the cost of each part of the project. Then at the bottom a grand total of four million seven hundred dollars, all paid from the Giles/Emerson foundation.

The bids were listed on the second sheet. There were only seven names on the list and each of them had put in a bid of well over the cost of the project. Osborne was listed as well, and at his name was the word "whatever." He stared at it for several seconds as he tried to understand. Then he got up and went to the rooms where the Feds were. He handed it to Towers.

"Hey. I just found this and thought you might like to see it." Towers took it and looked it over, going over each sheet in the file. "I had Allen pull all the things from the big cabinet in my office. Most of it was crap but I've been going through it. This was in it. I didn't even see it until now."

"Is this a copy?" Luke had no idea and said so. "If this is the original — and I've no doubt that it might be — then this is what we've been looking for. It says a lot for what was going on here. And the fucking *whatever* is enough to have all of them convicted."

When Towers picked up his phone, Luke went back to his office. Allen was on the phone so he bypassed him for his own office. As soon as he sat down he felt Jack's anger. Luke was grabbing up his jacket when she spoke.

I might be in jail soon. He leaned against his desk and asked her why. *Because my father is going to make me kill him. He's all up in arms about Slone. I swear to you, I want to be just like her someday. She is awesome.*

That she is. Do you need me to come down there and show you how awesome I am? She giggled and he relaxed. *Or when we get home we could go play in the woods and I could chase you down for a good fuck.*

A good long fuck would be nice. He felt his cock lengthen and had to adjust himself. *Do you have any idea how much I love having sex with you? Having you eat me and fuck me like you do?*

You're killing me right now. She laughed. *You shouldn't be doing this to me like this. I have Feds in the other room, and I'm pretty sure if you get too aroused, Slone will know it.*

She told me about that. Not that she could smell me but that you could. I'm learning all sorts of things from her. And about whelping a child. He sat down and thought again about her with his baby. *Do you mind if we wait for a few months before I get pregnant? It seems my husband to be has gotten me a job.*

Whatever you need, love. And you need this. We both need it. If for nothing else than to have a place where I can run across the street to see you. She told him she and Slone had seen it this morning. *What do you think? Can you work there?*

I can. The only thing I can see is that it's going to be expensive. I mean, just the lighting alone will be horrendous. And don't tell me its fine. I need to show a profit at some point, and too much overhead isn't going to make that happen.

He didn't say anything, knowing she was right. They chatted a little more and then he closed the connection, asking for her promise that if she had to go to jail, she'd call him first. She said she'd try. Luke sat at his desk again and got to work. The sooner he was finished here, the sooner he could go home to his future wife.

~~~

"This meeting is private." Mark tried for the third time to get rid of the other woman. It was bad enough that he had to meet with the daughter, but to have this woman here was too much. "Should you like to wait in the car? I'm sure we won't be long."

"I'm not going anywhere, so get on with it." Mark wanted to slap her…just reach across the table and smack that look off her face. But he didn't want to make a scene. And he was pretty sure that she'd try to hit him back. "I'm here because we have plans after this meeting. And I'm hungry."

Mark looked at his daughter. She was smiling at the woman as if she were the greatest thing in the world, and that pissed him off. He slammed his fist onto the table and made her look at him. It had worked when she'd been younger…had her cowering in the chair afraid for her life. And she well should have been now. But she looked at him as if she were bored, and more than that, she looked as if she didn't care what he had to say. This insolence was going to end right now.

"You're going to stop this foolishness and bring that brother of yours to heel. I want you both home now. I've given you enough to hang yourself on, and now that you're unemployed and homeless, I'll take you back." She shook her head and he felt his temper rise. "Daughter, I've had enough of this. Do as I say."

"It's Jack. Or Jacklyn if you want. You can say it if you want. But it will not change the fact that I'm an adult and I have been making decisions on my own for a great many years. And so you know, not only am I not unemployed, but I have my own business. A man who loves me too. You, however, can go right to hell. I'm through with you as of the moment you threatened my friend." He curled his hand into a fist and was lifting it from the table when she spoke again. "You even draw that back, it will be the last of many horrible decisions you've made regarding me. I will guarantee it."

"You'll not take that tone with me." Mark was afraid, terrified of her all of a sudden, but he knew to show fear would be the end of this and his plans. "I will not tell you again that you're to do as I say. I don't care how old you are. If you do not listen to me, I will tell the world what you really are."

She said nothing. Mark looked over at the other woman and smiled. He knew that he had her, that his daughter would bow before his wishes and be home before he had to resort to doing as he'd threatened to do for years. Going to the paper. Not that he'd do it, but it was a lovely way to make her bend to his will. To have it public would bring in investigators and that would not do. Not for his daughter, but for him. He was the guilty party in all that had happened.

"Did she tell you that she killed a man? That in cold blood she killed a friend of mine as he sat in my kitchen drinking a fine glass of wine?" The woman only stared at him, so he knew that she was interested. "Dave and I were school hood chums. We'd been having dinner together for years and years. And then one night, in a fit of rage, she cuts open his throat and kills him."

"Oh my." The woman looked aghast and Mark smiled hugely. "What did the police say when they got there? I mean, it was murder, wasn't it? I'd think she'd still be in prison for it."

"Oh, we didn't call them. It was better that way. Her mother had been ill for a very long time, and the thought of losing Daughter to prison in such a manner was too much for me. I know now that I should have done things differently, but, well....” Mark leaned back in his chair. “So we buried him. Hid his body away so that her instability would never be questioned. And now I must insist that she come back to our home so that I can keep an eye on her. You never know what will set her off.”

“No, I don’t think you could.” Mark looked at his daughter, who was staring at him with so much hatred that he wanted to bask in it. When the woman spoke again, he looked at her and waited for her to tell him that she would help her pack his daughter up. “I would guess that the fact that you sold her to the man, this childhood friend of yours, for a hundred bucks would be something that would make her murder him. I would have murdered you both, but she was young.”

“What are you talking about?” He looked over at his daughter and wondered what she’d found out. “Sold her to him indeed. He had a thing for young men, not women.”

“Oh, that’s right. You sold Allen to him. And he’d been fucking the poor young boy for years. It was why he came over on Friday nights. To get his rocks off on an eleven-year-old. But Jack found out, didn’t she? Found the man sodomizing her brother, and she did go a little mad. And she did kill him. But not before you tried to kill her.”

“This is insanity.” He stood up, only to be told to sit down. The man in his head was telling him that if he moved again, if he so much as tried to leave, he would hunt him down. “You’re lying. I don’t know what you think you know, but it’s all lies.”

“And he’s not dead, is he?” Mark felt his heart pound hard in his chest as his daughter spoke. “Dave has been living it up on the insurance you claimed for him when he went missing for more than seven years. Shame, really, that he's going to be caught. And I'm pretty sure that whatever they give him will not be enough to make up for all the years you made Allen suffer. Because he did, you worthless piece of shit."

Mark looked at the doorway. It was too much for him...his daughter knew entirely too much for her own good. "I'm going to call the police as soon as I leave this establishment. You'll hear from my —"

"I don't think so." The man that sat down put his hand on the table and that was all, just his hand. Mark felt his bladder start to panic, the feeling of being too full and too afraid at the same time. He would not wet himself, but he was very close. "You've been a very bad boy, haven't you Mark? Or should I call you Anthony? Nice ring to it. Anyway, I've been digging around in that head of yours, and I have to tell you, you're one fucked up individual, aren't you?"

"Do I know you?" He looked at his daughter and wondered what else she might have told these two when she looked at him, then back at the man.

"You know my father?" The stranger nodded and she looked at Mark. "Does he know what sort of individual you are? What a sick motherfucking bastard you are?"

"I don't know him." The man nodded at him and smiled at his daughter. "I would like to leave now." They all ignored him and Mark started to stand. But the man pointed to the chair and he found himself seated again against his will.

"No, he doesn't know me, or I him. Not really. I was just in the right place at the right time. I saw him in the airport and he...well, he touched me. Sometimes that's all it takes, just a touch, and I can find out a great deal about a person. But in addition to touching him, I had myself a little taste of his blood too." Mark put his hand over the small mark on his neck. He'd noticed it just after he'd gotten off the plane. "Yeah, that's the spot. You should have better care who you let drink from you. All sorts of secrets come to light."

"You bit me?" The man nodded and leaned back. "You can't do that. You can't just bite someone and get away with it."

"You can't expect to treat your children the way you have and get away with it either, but you do, don't you?" The man smiled at him and Mark felt his bladder simply let go. He felt his urine run down his leg and into his shoes before he could think. Fangs. The man had large, long and sharp fangs. "I see you've figured out that I can bite whom I please."

"What do you want?" When the man smiled again, Mark had to tighten his ass. He was going to mess himself next and if he did, Mark knew that the world would know it. "I don't want you near me."

"Now, isn't that just too fucking bad?" The man looked over at his daughter and the woman. "I'm Steward Thomas. I'm a friend of Dan Rogers."

Mark stood up. He no longer cared that anyone saw him. He wanted nothing to do with his daughter, and his son could go straight to hell, where he was more than likely headed anyway. As soon as he was cleared of the table, the man spoke again.

"You can run, but you'll never be free of me. I've a taste of you now and you will forever be hearing from me." Mark nearly ran from the room, the man's laughter still echoing in his head.

Going into his room and closing the door, Mark leaned against it as he tried to think. They were going to expose him, he thought, and his daughter would be right out there telling them what had really happened that day. And many days after too. He'd used the fact that she thought she'd killed Dave and had abused her for many hours, enjoying it the entire time because Dave had been close enough to hear, had even recorded her screams a few times. Mark didn't know what he'd done with the recordings, but was sure that he'd used them sexually.

He pulled his phone from his pocket and tried three times to dial Dave's number. It wasn't until he heard his friend's raspy voice that he felt the hysteria bubbling up. He had to put his hand over his mouth twice when his terror got the better of him.

"She knows. Daughter knows what happened. They might be coming for you." There was a garbled response, then nothing. "Dave, did you hear me? Daughter knows, and it's only a matter of time before she tells someone who might come after you."

"Mr. Wagner?" The voice, eerily low, asked him twice more if he was Wagner. "It will do you no good to deny it. Dave here has confirmed who you are. We're sending someone for you. Or they may already be there. I'm not sure when our boss called them."

The door behind him nearly rattled off the hinges when someone knocked. His whimper must have gone over the line because the person at the other end laughed. Backing away from the door, he watched as the door knob turned and the door slowly opened. Mark dropped to his knees just as the three men in suits came in. The fight with his sphincter ended in a loss, and he felt his bowels let go just as his bladder had.

"Mr. Anthony Wagner? We have a warrant for your arrest." Mark didn't ask him for what, he knew his list was long. But the man started spouting off things as he pulled his arms behind him and put on the strip of plastic. "Murder, attempted murder, insurance fraud, tax evasion, kidnapping...."

Mark tuned him out. The man in front of him smiled, and Mark had a feeling he was never going to see the inside of a court room. His fangs were just as lethal looking as Steward's had been.

"You're going to pay for your bad choices in life." Mark nodded at him. "Do you have any idea how much fun we're going to have with you before we're finished? Loads and loads. More than you ever had when you were torturing your children. And I have it on good authority that you're going to whimper and cry like a little child. Just the way you are now."

"I was a good father." The man threw back his head and laughed. "Why can't you just let me go? I have money. I will give it all to you if you simply let me go."

"You haven't a pot to piss in and we all know it. And about now, your little girl is finding out that everything your wife left her is now in ruin." He stepped back when Mark was lifted from the floor. "You really should have thought this whole thing through. Did you think that she'd just let you take her back there to wait on you hand and foot? Or are you stupid enough to think that no one would miss her or her brother when you killed them? That was the plan, wasn't it, Wagner? You were going to use them for as long as you could, then kill them. You are going to pay for a lot of damage you caused."

"She's my daughter and she should take care of me." The man laughed, and Mark was led away. "What's going to happen to me now? Where are they taking me? To jail?"

"Nope." He was being moved down the hall when the man finally answered. "You're going to be our play thing now. Steward told us that we could do with you what we wanted for as long as you lived. And we're going to make sure you live to be a very old man."

As the elevator doors closed, it occurred to Mark what he meant. He started screaming the moment the closed space began to descend. He was still screaming for them to let him go, begging for it when he was led out of the building and into the awaiting car. Mark knew then that he was going to die. But he had a feeling it wasn't going to be soon enough. Not nearly soon enough for him.

Chapter 11

"And just how do you figure into this thing with my sire? You aren't his friend, so what the hell are you?" Jack watched the man as he sat there after her father left. He and Slone made small talk, but she was so stunned with seeing her father fall apart that she didn't pay much attention. "You're someone that knows him. And a little of what happened that night, so who are you?"

"I'm Steward Thomas." She nodded and he smiled again, and this time she saw them. "I'm a very old and bored vampire. And a friend of your mate. Luke and I have...conversed over the years about his speculation of having a mate."

"And what does that have to do with this?" He only smiled more. "You're an ass, aren't you? I mean, I thank you for what you did just now, but you're an ass."

"I've been called worse." She was sure he had and said as much to him. "You should know that he won't bother you again. I've done things to insure that."

"I had no intentions of letting him bother me now. And you didn't answer me. What does this have to do with you?" He glanced at Slone, who simply got up and moved away from the table. She took her purse and her light jacket but said nothing as she moved away. "Did you do that?"

As soon as he nodded, she punched him in the face. Blood erupted from his nose and lip and she was shocked at herself. When he glared at her, she sat very still wondering what the hell had gotten into her. Then he did the strangest thing. He laughed. And laughed hard.

"Luke said that you were a fire cracker. Not his exact words, mind you, but close enough. He also said that you'd be pissed at me. I think I'm going to like you, Jacklyn Emerson." Jack nodded, not sure what to say to him. "I did this not just for you, but for your brother. Did he ever tell you that he met me?"

"No. He never mentioned you. But then I've not had a lot to do with him for a while." Steward nodded and leaned back in the chair. "Are you going to tell me or make me have to hit you again?"

"You won't hit me. You are appalled that you did it the first time. You are not, my dear, a violent person. But yes, I'll tell you." He waited while the waiter asked her if she was ready to order, and when she told him what she wanted, he walked away. "He and I stumbled across one another in a jail cell. The day you left him."

Jack felt her heart twist and hurt again for what she'd done to her brother. Even after all these years she wanted to go back and do what he wanted. But Steward continued before she could dive deeper into her *what if's* and *I should have's*.

"You did the right thing. And even that night, he knew it." She shook her head. "I can tell you that he did. I sort of...let's just say I gave him a great deal to think about. And when I touched his mind, I knew that, like you suspected, that he'd been hurt a great deal more than you knew for sure. He had been hurt by that man."

"He never told me. I only...the night that I walked in on my father and Mr. Patrick talking about it is when I knew for sure. I think it's what got my brother into drugs in the first place." Steward nodded, then shook his head. "I don't understand."

"The rapes were the reason he turned to drugs, but it's not why he was into them so heavily. That too was of your father's making. He bought them for him, supplied them for him, and even when Allen was too stoned to take them himself, he fed them to him. I think he was being subsidized to care for an addicted child. And he didn't want to lose all that extra income, I guess. Your father should have been dead long ago." Jack felt the tears roll down her face. She'd left him to that. "Don't think of it that way. Had you not left him, I would never have found him. And getting him into the proper places was what I did for him. Your brother is a good man. And I was very glad to help him."

"I owe you for that." He shook his head, and she nodded. "I do. Had it not been for you, he'd be dead. He'd be...there was so much going on when I left. The pain of it all. I just couldn't take it any longer."

"No, neither of you could. And you leaving saved you both. I was just the one who could help him. And today, I was able to help you." She asked him why. "I don't have to have a reason, do I?"

"If you expect me to be okay with this, you will." The waiter brought her the sandwich she'd ordered, and she found that her appetite had fled. Pushing it back, she looked at Steward and waited. He'd tell her or not, but she hoped that he would.

"All right. One night about thirty-five years ago, I met a lovely young woman. She was pretty in the way that you're beautiful. Long dark hair, the grayest eyes I'd ever seen, and a heart as pure as the snow we found ourselves in. She was your mother." Jack wanted to tell him that it couldn't have been her mother, as she'd been only a teenager that long ago. But she knew that her mom would have been in her early twenties and she would have already been married to her father. "You're doing the math, aren't you?"

"She talked about you. Not you but someone." He nodded and smiled. "She said that even a stranger would be kinder to her than her own husband. And that sometimes regret can make you do the dumbest things. It was you, wasn't it?"

"Yes. We had a one night stand. A single night of paradise that has lived in my heart for all this time. And then, all the way back then, I knew that I'd find her again someday, and I did. Through her children. I loved your mother with all my heart." Jack thought of Luke and her love for him and wondered if it was the same. "She was my mate but she was with another. I would have taken her that night, but in my arrogance, I thought she'd be there forever. Then things were set in motion that tore us apart. It wasn't until I met your brother in that cell that I realized she was gone."

"She never stopped loving you." Steward nodded. "You should have taken her. You might have saved her life."

Jack wasn't blaming him for her mother's death but wanted her to have been happy, even for a time. But Steward shook his head and looked around the room before he said anything more.

"She said that our love, our need was for people in fairy tales. That the kind of thing we had, a night of passion and promises, was for people who did not exist but who would live out their lives in our minds. I didn't work hard to convince her otherwise. I knew what she was to me, but as a vampire who had lived for so long, I just never thought of her as dying. Or someone who would get sick. I assumed she'd always be there for me. I was wrong." He turned back to her. "I'm not your parent, nor would I ever assume to order you around as one would, but you and your brother have a second chance at this. A chance to get your lives together in a way she would have been proud of."

"I'm working on it." He nodded and stood up. "Are you going to be around? A part of this life we now have? I'd very much like for you to be. If only you can show up on occasion to visit."

"I'd very much like that." As he moved by her, he asked her for a single kiss. "I won't take what you do not offer freely, but with a kiss I can take enough of you into me to help should you need it."

She stood up and offered him her wrist. He looked at it, then at her. She knew what she was doing, and that Luke might not be happy about it, but she wanted the man in her life that had made her mother have a shy smile once in a while. He leaned over and bit gently. Then when he lifted his head, he smiled at her.

"Your mate will want to mark you the moment he sees you." She laughed as she tossed money on the table. "Ah, I see. You're counting on this."

"No, but now that you mention it, I think I am." As they left the restaurant she looked at the courthouse just down the block. "In fact, I think I'll go and see if he's ready to get a start on that now."

"Good luck to you, my dear. You are more like your mother than I had first thought. As is Allen. The two of you will be a good team." Then he bowed before her and disappeared. Jack moved down the street thinking about her mate and what she was going to do to him even as she started thinking of ways to get Allen out of the office for a while. She was so going to enjoy this.

~~~

Luke started to tell Allen that he wanted him to go home for the day. He'd been in and out of his office so many times that he was limping badly and he looked like he was in a great deal of pain. But when he saw Jack standing there, he leaned back in his chair until it protested.

"You finished with your father?" She nodded and moved into the room, closing the door behind her. "I take it things went well. He's going back to his lonely home all by himself."

"I have no idea where he's going, but I doubt it will be home. I had a very interesting lunch with Steward Thomas. He said you know him." Luke nodded and nearly whimpered when he heard the lock engage on the door. "Did you know that he knew my family? Long before he met my father?"

"No." She took off her jacket and tossed it in the general direction of the couch. Then she kicked off her shoes as she made her way across his office. "Allen should go home, don't you think?"

"I already sent him there. He's in a great deal of pain." The buttons on her blouse were opened slowly, but she didn't open her blouse as she went, leaving it closed so that all he got were glimpses of what was beneath. "I've been a bad wolf. And I've been told that you're going to need to mark me again. And soon."

She put out her wrist and he could smell the vampire on her. He wanted to demand her to tell him where he was, but Luke had a feeling this was going to be much more fun. He growled low when she moved her wrist over his mouth, and then he licked her. Her moan had him adjusting his cock.

"Do you know what it means to mark you? I'm going to have to be very thorough about it. I might have to mark you in more than one place." Her laughter, sexy and warm, seemed to float over him. "Come here, Jack. I want to taste you."

"I'd like to suck your cock first. Take you into my mouth and feel the way you fuck me down the back of my throat." She moved around his desk and pulled his chair out. "Put your hands on your chair, Luke. I want to play."

He did as she commanded and then watched her drop to her knees. He felt his cock fill as she reached for his belt. Before she had his pants opened, he knew that as soon as she touched him he was going to come. He only hoped that he'd be able to fuck her like he wanted when she was finished.

"You are going to have to let me have my fun too." She told him she was counting in it. "Christ."

His dick was free but not for long. As soon as he was freed from one confined place, she put him into another, but her hot, wet mouth was much better than his briefs. He nearly cupped the back of her head to guide her to how he wanted her to take him, but her low growl had him stop. She told him to not touch her or she'd leave him just like he was. He was pretty sure that she'd do it too. Simply get up and leave him hard and aching.

Luke had had oral sex before. And right now, with Jack between his legs sucking him like she was, he knew that that's all it had been before, oral sex. This was a mind-blowing motherfucking blow job, and his entire body was feeling her. He rocked his hips up as she swallowed him down, moaned when she rolled his balls, full and hot, into her hand. Luke started to beg, plead with her to let him take her. But she only continued what she was doing, torturing him until he thought he'd go completely insane.

No. I need this. He growled, and her laughter echoed in his mind. *Are you going to come down my throat, love? Let me taste you as you fill my mouth, give me all that you have. Come for me, Luke. Come now.*

Luke gripped the arms of his chair and exploded in her mouth. He watched her bob her head over him, take him as deep as she could as he felt his balls fill again. Pulling her away from him, his cum still dripping from the tip, he stood her up. Then he pushed her back over his desk and tore her pants from her. Her scent nearly pulled his wolf. He wanted her too, wanted to taste the hot cream that was all theirs.

He slammed into her heat, coming again, and his balls seemed to fill again almost as soon as he emptied them. As she tightened around him, milked him with her sheath, he ripped her small silky bra and took her breast as deeply into his mouth as he could. Biting down on her, tasting her blood, he roared around her as he emptied himself into her again. Her teeth sinking into his shoulder, tearing into his flesh made his vision blur. When she screamed around her bite, Luke felt his world tilt on its axis as he dropped onto her. She'd killed him was his last thought.

He knew that he'd passed out. For how long was anyone's guess, but when he lifted his head and looked down at Jack, she smiled at him and wrapped her arms around his neck. He kissed her on her mouth before she could speak.

"I love you." She nodded and told him she loved him as well. "I've never, not in all my life, come that hard. You are a temptress and an amazing woman. And I know that I have never lost consciousness before. You have humbled me in the sex department."

"I'm just that good." He stood up and lifted her with him. As he sat down, he held her to him. Her body straddled his and her naked breasts were right where he could nibble. "You do know that I have nothing to wear home, right? I mean, not one stitch of clothing."

"Works for me." She smacked him on the head. "You could just shift and run home. I might join you in that. It's been a very strange day. A good run might make things a little easier to handle for us both."

"I'm still not very comfortable with being a wolf." He knew that. But every time she shifted, she got a little more relaxed about it. "What if you just gave me one of your shirts and I wear it like a dress until we get to your car?"

"I don't have anything here either. Maybe, with you being right across the street, we should think about leaving extras around. Might save us a bit of embarrassment." She nodded and laid her head on his shoulder.

"I think my father is dead." Luke said nothing because if he was gone and Steward was involved, he was more than likely going to suffer a while before he was dead. "Steward told me that I'd not be bothered by him again. That Allen and I had a second chance in our lives. Do you suppose…I wonder if Father will know just how badly he hurt us?"

"I'm sure he does now." As she sat up and looked down at him, he decided to tell her what he knew. "Steward is a good man. A wonderful friend, but he does not take well to people who are abusive. It matters little if they're human or animal. He is swift and just in his treatment of them."

She stared at him for several seconds. Luke was worried that she'd ask him what sort of treatment that Steward would employ. "He told me something. Steward said that…he told me that he wanted to stay in our lives. I actually invited him to do so."

"Good." Luke waited, knowing there would be more. When she was quiet for so long, he wondered if she'd fallen asleep, but her heavy sigh had him pulling her closer to him.

"He knew my brother and mother." As she explained what Steward had told her, Luke started seeing the pieces of his friend fall into place. He'd often wondered why he was always so sad, wondered too if the man had ever loved. Now he knew the reason for both.

"He's been around, our friend in so many ways, for nearly all my life. My dad knew him as well. They were great friends at one time, then something happened. I'll have to tell Dad about your mom. He'll be glad to know that he'd not done anything to upset their friendship." Kissing her on the mouth, he looked up at her. "We should really get home. I heard from Audra and she said that she would have dinner ready for us at six. It's just after five now."

As they tried to figure out what she could wear, Luke thought of Steward. He'd taken Jack's blood. And while he wasn't pissed about it, knowing that the man would do nothing to harm either of them, he did wonder why. Was it because he felt responsible for her? And Allen?

I'm not that nice of a guy. Luke smiled as Steward touched his mind. *I hope you don't mind, but there is a package that you and Jack might be able to use about now. That pretty girl of yours had a twinkle in her eye when she left me. I thought that with your nature and her need to be with you, that clothing safety would be the furthest thing on your minds. Oh, and I'm watching over Allen. He has problems coming his way and I want to be there for him. Because I like him, not because I feel any responsibility toward him.*

Luke went to his office door and opened it as he answered Steward. He handed the large blue bag to Jack and sat down to watch her go through it. The man had good taste, he'd give him that. The blouse and short skirt was something that he might have picked out for her. And the little jacket fit nicely over her rounded breasts. Luke had to think of something else or these clothes would be trash as well.

Where are you staying? I don't have a lair for you as yet, but I will put one in if you're going to be around for a bit. And I'm assuming that since you took Jack's blood, you will be. Plus, she said that she wants you here. And I, for one, would listen to her. She's a bit on the temperamental side when she doesn't get her way. He growled, and Luke laughed. *She gave it to you freely or you'd be a dead man right now, and we both know it. She's very strong.*

Did she tell you that she hit me? Luke started laughing and had to tell Jack what he and Steward were talking about. *I don't think it's all that funny. I'm not saying I didn't deserve it, but she punched me in the mouth and bloodied my nose too. I didn't see it coming at all. And that's a good thing for her, not so much for me. And do not tell her, but I rather enjoyed it. She threw me off. Not many would live to talk about doing that to me.*

Like I said, she's very strong. When Jack was dressed and sitting on his desk, Luke felt his hunger for her rise up again. But he knew if he tore these from her, she'd hurt him. And as much as it would be fun, he was hungry for food too. He asked Steward what sort of trouble Allen was in.

He's walking home. I'm assuming that you offered him a car? He told him that Allen didn't drive but didn't go into details as to why. Steward seemed to understand. *There's a man following him. Only a human, but with our young man hurt like he is, I don't think he'd stand much of a chance against him. So I'm keeping an eye on him.* He was quiet for a moment, and Luke started to speak when Steward did.

They were moving out to her car when Steward spoke again. The wolf in him wanted to shift and run to the younger man. But he held Jack back from getting into her car. If they had to go, he wanted to be the driver.

The man that is following him has others with him. Their intent on the young human is not good. There are five, maybe six here. The leader, if one would call him that, is the law here. Two of the men with him are dressed in their uniform. Luke pulled Jack to his car; his need to go was pounding at him. *Silver. I smell a great deal of silver on the men.*

The house he's living in is on pack land. He'll be protected by them. Steward told him he could see the wolves now. *They belong to Slone. But she's not aware that she's their alpha. I've tried to tell her, but she tells me they're her friends. The pack master, a big black wolf, would kill for her. And I mean even Hunter if he hurt her.* Luke had been surprised to know that the big wolf also slept outside the house nightly too. He protected what was his. *She's breeding, and he's never too far from her now. I think he knows.*

He more than likely does. Wolves, males of any kind, will know to protect her. She is a woman of great value to them. Not only because she does protect them, but she has an ability to speak to them as if she is one of them. Very commendable on her part. I'm thinking that, for the fact that he can more than likely smell Jack on me, I'd be wolf food. Luke doubted that. Steward would kill him before he leapt at him. *Luke, you should perhaps come to the house. The young man will need you very soon.*

His voice was calm; his words, however, were eerily frightening. *We're coming now. Jack and I are in my car and coming. We should be there very soon. And I'm going to have Hunter come as well. He'll be there faster as he lives closer than we are.*

When Steward told him that was a good idea, fear raced over him, and his wolf snarled to be let free. As soon as Steward told him he'd be waiting, Luke looked over at Jack. He knew she had felt his fear.

"Your brother is in trouble." She nodded. Her wolf moved along her skin as his had. "Steward is with him, but he wants us to hurry. I'm calling the others too. They'll be there before us. Hunter will protect him until we get there."

"What is it?" He told her he didn't know. "I don't want anything to happen to him. I just got him back. I love him. If anyone dares to…I'm not sure how I'll react, but this wolf in me wants to kill whoever touches him."

"I understand completely. My wolf is wanting to run to him, but this is better. Steward won't let anything happen to him." As they drove like they were being chased, Luke thought of the million and one things that could happen to his future brother-in-law. The other men, besides the chief, was it Osborne and some of his minions? Did Granger decide to get to them through Allen again?

He was so afraid for the young man that Luke had to stop thinking for just a second to take several deep breaths. Luke reached for his family.

Go to Allen, now. They all responded that they were leaving immediately. His dad said he was the closest and that he'd be there soon. *Steward is there. He's going to keep an eye on him until we get there. There are several men with Granger, and Steward can smell silver. So please be careful. And, Christ, please protect him.*

We will. He's our brother as much as you are. We'll take care of him. Hunter told him to take care getting there as well. And he told him that Slone was calling the troops. *She's had her wolves there too. I'm sure they will help. I don't know how she does it, but she can get them to do whatever she needs.*

Luke was pulling onto the road that would lead him to pack land when something occurred to him. He wondered if Allen had a weapon, and he wondered if he knew how to use it. As soon as this was over, he was going to have to sit down with him and find out if he wanted to be converted too. He would stand a better chance at this if he did.

"When this is done and he's all right, I'm going to have someone change him into a wolf. I don't want this to happen to him again." Luke looked at Jack when she spoke. "I know that I'm not comfortable with being one, but I know that if need be, I can kick some serious ass. He will be able to as well. I don't want anything to happen to him."

"I was thinking the same thing." And he hoped that he'd have the chance to talk to Allen about it too. Luke had never been so afraid in his life for a human. He knew that at all costs his family would protect him, but that didn't lessen his worry.

Chapter 12

Allen knew that he was being followed. He'd seen the man, two of them really, off and on since he'd left the office. The closer one of the two had even followed him into the store when he'd wandered in for something for dinner. The other man, bigger than the first, had stayed outside. And there was something about him that made Allen think he was helping rather than going to hurt him. His bag of food, whatever he'd bought, weighed heavily in his hand. Allen wondered if he could use it as a weapon and laughed at himself. *Sure, and I'll whip out my Glock and blow them all away too.* Allen wouldn't even know how to take the safety off of the stupid thing if he had one, much less kill someone with it.

The path to his new house wasn't long, but it was also full of places he knew that he could be jumped. Trees lined both sides of it with a lot of underbrush and vines. There was a stone wall at one place, long since fallen over in places, but there was enough of it left for a person or wolf, if that was what was behind him, to hide behind. Allen tried not to think about what was going to jump out at him.

Wishing that he'd taken the car that had been offered to him for rides back and forth to work, Allen paused to look at a group of trees. The man ducked behind a tree just as Allen looked his way. The other man stood in the lane for several seconds before he simply disappeared. His feeling that the man was there to help him was more profound now. Whoever he was, he just hoped he was in better shape than he was. If not, they were both dead.

You're not going to die and neither am I. You'll be fine if you listen to me. The voice echoed in his head and for whatever reason, he wasn't surprised. *We've talked before, you and I. Both verbally and through our link. I will explain later but for now, I'd like for you to trust me. Would you give me the benefit of the doubt and let me help you?*

I have no idea why, but I do. The man thanked him. *Can you contact my sister? I don't...if something should happen to me, I'd like to have her close. We've not been close for a number of years, but just lately we've...could you contact her for me?*

She and the others are on their way. Allen felt relieved and thanked the man. *The others, the pack, they're coming as well. If you see wolves, just be leery, but don't run from them. Wolves, like most animals of prey, enjoy chasing their meal. While I don't think they'd actually eat you, there is no reason to tempt them. There are pack and wild coming to help, and the man behind you is wolf too.*

I'm not even going to think about what you said about them maybe eating me. But I would ask you, who are you and why are you helping me? The man laughed. *I really need something else to think about other than I might die out here. I'm not normally such a pussy, but I'm beaten to shit and I'm not very strong. Please?*

You're as strong as you need to be and you're not being a pussy. Most men, hurt or not, would have run. You've done well in that you knew they were following you, yet you have not been stupid enough to confront them. *That is the sign of a smart man, not a dead one. Move again so that I can pinpoint your attacker.* Allen turned to move up the lane again and saw the big wolf. He nearly stopped but kept going. *You're going to be fine. Hunter and the pack is about to your home; the wild wolves are all along the path you take. The one in front of you will cause you no harm. Your sister and her mate are coming behind me and will be to you shortly. Are you armed, by any chance?*

No. I'm not...I don't own a gun. I don't even know how to fire one. The man told him he needed to learn. *Will I live long enough to learn that trick? And if you don't think I will, please lie to me and say it will be all right.*

I cannot lie to you, Allen. And you will be all right. Nodding to himself mostly, Allen kept walking. The closer he got to his house, the more of the wolf he could see. And he also knew that it wasn't the same one he'd seen along the road just a few minutes ago. Some were darker, others as light as snow. As soon as his house came fully into view, he noticed the huge wolf lying on the deck. The man in his mind spoke again before he could ask him if it was safe. *That would be Hunter. You should go to him as if you have had him there for weeks. He said to tell you that you're doing well. Do you need to be reassured, Allen?*

No. Yes. I don't think I know. Are you going to come closer now? He said no. *I see. And me and Hunter, we're going to do what is necessary to keep me safe?*

The laughter made him smile a little. The man, whoever he was, told him he'd be fine. Moving up onto the deck, he put his hand on the head of the wolf and was surprised at how soft he was. As soon as he pulled his hand back, the wolf snapped his teeth into his hand and drew blood. Allen wanted to run then. Simply drop his bag or hit him with it and run as fast and as hard as his semi-broken body would allow. But before he could make his feet move in the general direction away from the sharp teeth, someone else spoke to him.

Hello. The wolf had bitten him and now…. Christ, he could hear Hunter now. *Don't freak out, okay?*

I have no intentions of doing so. But I should like to talk to you about becoming a wolf. All this human stuff I'm going through is quite painful. The sooner the better too. Hunter laughed and told him he'd do it. *Thank you. I know you have to hurt me badly, but right now, I'm thinking it won't be as bad as the man behind me is going to do.*

There are several, but he is the only wolf. And of the five he had with him, only four remain. Well, now only three. My brothers are taking care of them now. As is your friend that has been speaking to you. Allen sat on the chair and wondered if he would be able to take care of someone if he needed to. Hunter stood up just as a man came out of the tree line. Now this man he knew.

"Got yourself a watchdog, did you? Good for you. But it won't do you no good. I'm still here and you're gonna listen to me." It was Granger, the chief, and he looked pleased with himself. "I've come to talk to you. Call the dogs off and we'll go inside and have us a little talk. Man to whatever the hell you are like." Even without Hunter's "*don't,*" he wouldn't have taken the guy into his house. He might be hurt, but he wasn't entirely stupid.

"I think we can speak from where we are. You stay over there and I'll be right here. What do you want, Granger? This is pack land, and if I remember my information correctly, you aren't supposed to be here unless invited. I didn't invite you; I'd remember if I did." Granger laughed and Allen wondered if the man knew how much like a braying ass he sounded. "I would like to suggest that you leave while you can. I'm not as unprepared as you seem to think I am."

"I'll just bet you think you are. And no, can't do that. We have a plan, me and my partner, and the sooner you're gone, the sooner them others will back off. Might even leave us all together. I'd like that right fine. We were doing just fine before them Emersons came sniffing around. And that bitch too. We had her just where we wanted her." Allen had to think for a moment who he meant.

"You mean Slone? What does she have to do with this meeting between you and me?" Allan watched the tree line and saw several wolves come out slowly. He wasn't really afraid any longer, but he was nervous about how this was going to go. "Slone has done nothing to you but supplied you with an endless amount of money for projects that never got finished. You and Osborne have been taking advantage of her for years."

"Yeah, we have. And as soon as you're dead, we'll do it again. See, you're going to be our crowning glory. As soon as your dead and torn up body is thrown on her door step, all smelling of them Emersons, she'll think they turned on her and she'll toss them out, and lock herself up again. We like it that way. Out of sight and out of mind. And the money will begin to flow again without all her nosing around in our business. How the hell somebody got her out in the first place…well, that's soup under the bridge now. So you and I are going to have a nice conversation. Then I'm going to kill you."

"How do you propose to do that? She'll be able to tell that her family didn't do anything to me. She's a wolf too, in case you forgot." Granger laughed, and Allen tried not to think about how callously he'd said he was going to kill him. Like it was something he did daily. "I don't think you've thought this through properly. You should simply leave and come up with a better plan. Go on, go away. Shoo."

Hunter snorted, and Allen thought it was a laugh. He glanced down at him and felt Hunter's head move under his fingers. Scratching him behind the ear, Hunter told him to keep him talking.

How the hell am I supposed to do that, he wondered. "Did you know that the men who came with you are all gone? I'm not sure that they're dead, but when I was told they were taken care of, I just assumed he meant dead. It would be the way I would do it. Kill them, I mean. Less to worry about later. Also, you should know that my family is coming. All of them." He was babbling and hated that. He didn't like it in others and certainly didn't in himself. But he was talking and that's what he'd been told to do.

"Your sister? Shit, she's nothing. Stupid little cunt that ain't got no business around here none anyway. Her daddy was going to take care of her. I thought he had it all in the bag. You too, but he's gone now. And nobody has heard from him since this afternoon. And that feller of hers, that other Emerson? We've got some nice plans for him too."

The car skidding to a stop near Granger had him backing up just enough not to get sprayed by gravel. Two men came out of the woods, but no one but Allen seemed to notice them. Luke moved around the car and stood near the front while Jack moved to stand in front of Granger as soon as she got out on her side.

"You're on private property. That's trespassing where I come from." Granger snorted and crossed his arms over his chest when Jack did the same. "You don't seem to be all that concerned that you're breaking the law. Why is that, I wonder? I thought it was because you don't care. But it can't be just that. I actually think you're just that stupid. I'm right, aren't I? You're just stupid."

"I'm smart enough to have gotten you here, now ain't I? And there ain't no law here that I don't control all by myself. Your pack law or whatever the hell you're calling it don't mean shit to me. Not to mention, you guys aren't that scary to me since I got me a lesson in how to take care of you. I have enough silver in my gun to take all three of you out when I start shooting, and I've put enough of the stuff on my skin that I damn near glow with it."

Allen watched as one of the men from the tree line simply disappeared. It was down to just Granger, he thought, and Allen wondered if he had any idea.

The silver was given to him by me. And it's not real. Well, other than it's silver in color. Your sister is correct, he is most stupid. Allen laughed at the man. *You should also know that all his cohorts are gone, dead, in the event you're wondering. Hunter will be taking care of their bodies when we are finished here. Could you do me a favor?*

Christ, anything. Allen heard the laughter and then saw the man come out of the woods. When he adjusted himself, Allen staggered back. In that moment he knew who the man was and where he'd met him before.

Stand up. Allen jerked up from the wall and stood stiff and slightly afraid. *Did I hurt you before? Did I do anything at all to you that you did not need? You are still alive, are you not, because I did you no harm other than to scare you senseless?*

No. But you threatened me. And you...you did save me. I thought of you every time that I thought of— The man laughed but it was bitter and cold. *I never touched anything after that. Not even a glass of wine with my dinner. You fucking terrified me.*

As was my plan. Now, for that favor. I wish for you to walk to Granger. He will not be able to harm you, but you need to take control from your sister. She is getting angry, and an angry she-wolf is an unreasonable one. If she is injured, the pack will surely tear him apart. And that simply will not do for what I have planned for him. Allen stepped off the porch and noticed that Hunter came with him. *Very good, Allen. Now when you are where you need to be, simply touch your sister's arm. It will calm her and give you the opportunity to talk to Granger. You'll know just what to say when you arrive.*

No, I won't. The man told him he would. *Is this going to get me killed? Is this your plan? To get me into a position that will get me dead?* As soon as the words left his mouth, he knew them to be untrue. The man had saved him and no matter how afraid he was of him, Allen knew that he'd never harm him.

Had I wanted you dead, Allen, you would have died long ago. Allen stopped moving as he considered his words. He had a feeling that the man wasn't talking about him killing Allen, but Allen doing it all on his own. Allen knew that he'd been headed down the road to his own demise. More so than he'd ever been. But the man, the one currently standing in the lane about thirty feet from him, had given him a terrifying idea of how he would have died. *Go to the man and talk to him. I trust you to finish this once and for all.*

As soon as he touched Jack's arm, she turned to look at him. The wolf was right there. He could see her, almost feel her as she moved along Jack's body. And he even saw the she-wolf reflected back at him when he looked into his sister's eyes. When she snarled but backed up, he turned to Granger.

Looking at the man, he could see two things almost at once. Granger was afraid. Terrified beyond what was going on right now, and he was high on something. Allen knew the look better than anyone. Granger was on something, and that alone gave Allen all the strength he needed to do this.

"Drugs slow your ability to make snap decisions, did you know that?" Granger snorted, and Allen saw the drop of blood at his nose. "Coke. Did you know that it was once my choice of drug to forget? Not that I forgot for long, but it did the trick for a time. But like all things, when it came to an end, the memories flooded back. And for some reason, they were worse than they were before. Do you find that to be true as well?"

"What the fuck are you talking about?" Granger wiped at his nose and looked at the blood. "This? You mean this? I can quit at any time I have to, but I like it too much. Yeah, boy, unlike you, I have willpower. And a lot of it. Then again, why should I give up something that makes me a king?" He pulled out his gun and waved it around.

"That will get you nowhere and fast. Do you want to know why? Because you're not a king. Not even a prince. All you are is a lowly jester, and not a very good one at that."

The gun fired, and Allen felt his body being pitched backward. He noticed that Granger was suddenly gone and the gun, still hot looking, lay in the dirt that he was falling into. Allen closed his eyes and decided that if he had to die, he was glad Jack was nearby. And he also wondered at the lack of pain from the shot and was grateful for it.

~~~

Jack watched her brother fall back. As she reached for him, a breath of hot air fell over her cheek and she turned to protect her fallen brother. But there was no one there, not even Granger. As she looked to the dirt and the gun, she leaned over to pick it up, but Luke stopped her.

"Fingerprints." She nodded and looked at Allen. It was then that she realized not only was he not bleeding, he didn't seem to be hurt at all. Jack stood up and kicked him in the foot. Allen moaned, but he didn't move other than to shift his feet away from her.

"Stop being a melodramatic pansy and get up." He looked up at her, and she smiled. "You're not hurt. Not even a scratch. I think the bullet went wide."

"He shot me." She shook her head. "I heard it. I can't believe he missed me. I'm...I'm not hurt? Really?"

Allen sat up, and Jack jerked him to her. She'd never been so happy to see him not hurt in her life. But when he moaned, she let him go and stepped back. She'd forgotten that he'd been hurt before. He smiled at her, the loopy grin she remembered from when they were kids, and she hugged him again. She really loved this guy.

Just then Steward seemed to shimmer into view. Allen took a hasty step back, but before she could tell him that this was the man who'd helped, Allen was pulled into his arms and held tightly by Steward. When he let him go, Jack could see that he was just as happy as she was that he was all right.

"You did very well." This time when he stepped back, Allen looked at the man. It was hard to say if he was pissed or not, but Steward threw back his head and laughed. Jack wondered what the hell was going on between the two of them. Then Steward looked at her.

"He is very smart, your brother. Allen wishes to know if I am marking him and if so, how does he keep his mate from smelling me on him. I have just assured him that she would love the scent." Jack was confused and said so. "I marked him long ago, as you know, but now he wishes to be converted to wolf. I wish it to be vampire, as I am, but he assures me that he would prefer a wolf. What say you, Hunter? Do you need another pack member? He will be a fine addition."

"And he's standing right here." Allen took another step back as he continued. "I've already spoken to Hunter, and he said that he'd do it. I'm sick of being the odd man out. I want to be able to bounce back as the rest of you have." Hunter, a man now dressed in tear-away pants, came walking toward them, pulling a shirt over his head. He grinned at her when she flushed.

"I would be proud to have him in this pack. We're going to sit down and talk about it, but I think he's got it straight in his head what he wants and what is going to have to happen. And he's right about being able to bounce back with the rest of us. I've never been so afraid for a puny human in my life." Hunter looked at her and winked. "You'll have to give me permission. I know that he's not in the same condition you were in when you were converted, but he is your blood and you're older than him. It's up to you if he is wolf or not."

Jack could only stare at Allen and wonder. This was her brother. The boy she'd left behind seemed to have grown up. It was stupid. Of course, he would grow up, but she was surprised at it all the same. But she had already decided, if it was possible. And if Allen wanted it, she'd agree. With a nod to them all from Jack, Hunter nodded and moved away with her brother, talking about all that had to be done. Jack stood there for several seconds before what was going to happen to him sunk in. Her brother would be just fine.

When Luke wrapped his arms around her, she leaned into him and asked Steward what had happened to Granger. She wasn't sure he was going to answer her, but when he did, he seemed to be slightly sad about his answer.

"He will no longer be an issue. None of the men at the stationhouse that were here today will be a concern for any of the good citizens of this town. I have taken care of their remains as well." Jack noticed a small drop of blood on his lip, and he licked at it. "I would hate to have a meal go to waste." Steward only grinned at her, and she nodded.

Jack shivered, and Luke tightened his hold on her. She had no idea why she thought that she didn't want any more details, but she was reasonably sure that if she got them, she'd have nightmares for the rest of her life. He nodded once to her before turning to talk to the rest of the Emerson men. Jack looked at Luke when he turned her in his arms.

"You have a meeting in an hour." She'd hoped that he'd forgotten about it. "And I have one with the Feds at my office. She's the woman that Towers said was investigating Osborne and his company. They have what they need to arrest Osborne, and they want me there in the event I can answer any questions she might have. Plenty, I'm sure, but I said I'd be there."

"I'll be fine. We're meeting at my building. And Audra and her son are going to be there as well." He asked her about the young man. "I hired him. With stipulations. He has to finish his last year of school, and if I can swing it, I'm going to help him with his college."

"There's a fund that Slone has set up that he will more than likely qualify for. It's an outreach program for underprivileged wolves to continue their education. You can ask Slone, but I'm pretty sure she'll say yes." Jack nodded and decided to talk to her as soon as this meeting was over. "Also, you should know that she and Hunter have ordered you a few supplies. Since you wouldn't take money for the art you did for them, they decided to help you out in other ways. You're going to have a fit about it and they know it. But I wanted you to have a heads up so it wouldn't freak you out before the meeting."

Jack tried to think why she'd be pissed but didn't comment. Luke led her to the car and was driving down the lane when she finally asked. It had cost her nothing but a few seconds of her time. What the hell could they have gotten her? He laughed before answering her. And that alone made her leery of going to her building.

"I don't know for sure. I do know that the truck arrived this morning and that three of the pack had to work all day to set it up." Jack felt her belly lurch up. "Calm down, honey. I'm sure it's not that much. Just a desk or two, I'm sure." But she had a feeling that it was more than that, a great deal more than that.

"It wasn't worth even one desk blotter, much less a single desk." As they pulled up in front of her building, she looked at him again. "What if he gets in there and Sweet starts realizing that I haven't a clue what I'm doing? What if the first thing he asks me, I puke all over him and he tells every living person he knows? I can't do this."

"Yes you can. You're very talented." He pulled her to him and kissed her. Everything but them and what his mouth was doing to her faded out. When he lifted his head, she was panting and he was smiling. "You don't puke on him and get the deal, I'll take you in the woods tonight, strip you down, and fuck you until you scream out my name."

"I do that anyway whenever you simply touch me." He laughed and kissed her again. "You're not giving me much of a goal. What I need is more of an incentive." Luke let her slip out of the car before he answered her.

"Your old boss called. Anderson. He wants you to come back to work for him. Begged me to tell you to call him as soon as possible. I said I'd think about it." She watched his face to see if he was kidding. "It seems that he's lost a great deal of business since you left him and is losing a lot more almost daily. Did you know that my father was one of his clients?"

"Your dad? For what?" Luke laughed and drove off. Jack decided right then that she was going to murder him when she got home. There was no way she was going to be able to think of anything else now but her old boss. Jack turned when someone said her name behind her. It was Josh, the young man she'd hired. He looked as nervous as she felt.

"They're here." She nodded and took a step toward him as he continued. "I had Mabel down at the diner bring in some cookies and stuff. She also threw in a big urn of coffee and some pitchers of her famous iced tea. I hope that was okay. I told her you'd settle up tomorrow. She said not to worry."

She nodded and stopped in front of him. "You look very nice. I guess I should have dressed up too."

His suit was a little worn, but it looked much better than the jeans and tee-shirt she had on. When she started to fuss with her hair, something she never did, he told her she looked great. She was sure the kid was going to be a heartbreaker when he got old enough to take woman seriously, if he ever did. Taking a deep breath, she moved toward what was going to be her office. She stopped in her moving so quickly that Josh bumped her from behind.

"They just got it set up before Mr. Sweet got here. And the guys put it together while I was still reading the box. Just like they knew how to do it." Jack was sure they did. Construction workers would simply know that slot *a* fit into hole *b* or whatever to put together a dozen cubicles as they'd done. With or without instructions. "I had them set up your desk near the window in your office. They said they could move it if you want. The rest of it I wasn't sure what to do with, so I had them just put the things together until you decided."

"The rest of the things? Just how many other things are there? You know what, I don't care right now. I have a meeting and I'm nervous enough without thinking about how much money I'm going to owe these people." She had a feeling she'd be hard pressed to get a total from them, much less be able to make a single payment. It was all she could do not to puke, as she'd told Luke she was going to do. "Is Mr. Sweet in there?"

Josh shook his head and pointed at the stairs. The large open space up there was going to be her employee break room, if she ever had more than just her and Josh. Josh started toward the stairs and she followed him. He was still talking but for the life of her, she couldn't hear him over the buzzing in her head. When he opened the door to the large room, what looked like a couple of dozen men were standing in the large room. And a huge shiny oak table had at least half that many more sitting at it.

There was no way on earth this was just Mr. Sweet's firm. She was so fucked.

"There you are." She took Mr. Sweet's hand when he pulled her into the room. "I hope you don't mind, but when I said I was meeting with you, a bunch of the other clients you had worked with decided to come along too. We've been hashing out details on what we want and how you're going to give it to us. Not that we're going to be in charge, but we figured we'd take turns in our demands and let you hash out how to make our dreams come true."

"I am?" Mr. Sweet nodded and laughed. "I'm a little...I'm a lot overwhelmed right now. I didn't expect this."

Mr. Emerson...Cash...took her hand into his when Mr. Sweet walked away. She looked at him like a lifeline. When she felt calmer, he nodded once to her and told her to have at it. Jack watched as the men, her potential clients, all sat around the table. Jack was going to kill Luke as soon as she thanked him.

"Good evening, everyone. Sorry I'm late, but I had some personal things to take care of." The men and women nodded and smiled. Jack took a deep breath and let it out slowly. "I hope you guys aren't too disappointed in this meeting. I only expected one person and I'm not prepared to...I'm slightly out of my element right now. I just opened my...well, that's not quite true. I haven't even opened my doors yet and have three clients more than I thought I would."

"Four." She looked at Cash. "Four, honey. Hunter and Slone, Ellis, Luke, and Sweet here, if he behaves himself. He does have a way about him that makes him seem a little bossy."

As they laughed, she felt Luke's love. She might want to kill him right now, but he'd given her more than she'd ever dreamed up. Picking up her notes she'd made the night before, she started going over what she hoped were good guidelines and company policies. Christ, she was going to fail big time. She just knew it.

Chapter 13

Luke tried to reach Jack several times, but all he hit was a wall. Even calling her on the phone had gotten him little to nothing in the way of information. Josh said the message was that she was really busy. Busy for five hours? Her meeting with Sweet should have been over hours ago. Now it was just before midnight and he was going to get her. Grabbing his keys, he was headed out the door when she came in.

Naked.

"I wanted to surprise you." Luke nodded. "I had a really good day and wanted to celebrate with you."

The wine bottle was laid on the table, and then she frowned at him. Luke was sure that he'd lost all ability to speak. As he tried for the third time, he reached down and cupped his suddenly aching balls. Her grin told him she'd noticed.

"I have nineteen new clients." She walked around the room until she was in front of the refrigerator. As soon as she bent over at the waist to look inside the now open door, he grabbed the chair back in front of him. "Would you like something to eat?"

Nodding, he watched her reach further into the deep ice box, and moaned when her nipples hardened. As she stood up and turned to him, he had to work very hard at lifting his eyes to her face. Luke should have known she'd pay him back for the meeting.

"I'm really hungry." He was too but not for what she might pull from the cabinets she was now searching through. "I was thinking that I'd like to have a sucker. A really big one. What do you think?"

"I need you." She only giggled but didn't turn around. "Jack, do you have any idea what you're doing to me right now? How much I just want to bend you over that counter and fuck you hard?"

"I do." She turned and put a bowl on the table, along with a box of cereal. "Do you have any idea what it was like to walk into that room filled with men and women that want me to work for them? How I felt when they told me I was going to be their advertising firm no matter what kind of rules I put before them?"

"No." He tried to reason with his fingers to let go of the chair, but they were not listening. He couldn't go to her until they loosened their grip. "I only knew about Sweet. The others showed up on their own. Dad said he was going to go. He even told me there might be one or two others if they could make it, but he never said anything about nineteen. Are you going to let me fuck you?"

Nodding, she sat down on the counter. Luke felt his cock, already straining at the zipper, seem to grow larger, and the pull of his pants was painful now. As he watched, her legs opened and he could see her pussy, all of it. And she was soaking wet.

"I'm very needy right now." He nodded, feeling like a simpleton. "Are you going to break the chair or are you going to come here and fuck me? I seem to remember you saying that you were going to fuck me."

"I want to eat you. I want to drink deeply of your pussy and lap at that hard clit of yours. I want to hear you scream, feel you flood my mouth. Christ, I need you." Her legs spread wider and now he could see her clit as it peaked from her soft folds. It seemed to beg to him to bite her. "I want to drink from you so deeply that when I fuck you, I'm going to come almost immediately."

"I need to come too." He nodded and finally freed his fingers. As he moved toward her, he pulled his shirt over his head and dropped it to her floor. "Stop moving."

He did, not sure what she wanted him to do next but whatever it was, he was up for it...so long as he could come, buried deep within her. When she told him to strip down, Luke unbuckled his belt and pulled it free of the loops one at a time as she watched. Her arousal was strong, scenting the air like a field of flowers did after a summer storm.

"My wolf wants his share. Have you any idea how hard he's moving along me to take a deep bite of you? How much he'd like to lick your pretty pussy?" His wolf snarled at him to hurry up. "Jack, let him taste you before he pulls himself forward before I can control him."

Leaning back on the counter, he watched her finger slide down her belly to her pussy. Luke swallowed three times before he remembered he had to breathe too. As soon as she slid her finger into her wet pussy, his wolf took him.

His wolf wasn't going to be nice about tasting her. Luke knew and understood that. He moved up between her thighs, and Luke thought for sure she was going to push him away. Instead she curled her fingers into his fur and pulled him to her. Luke nearly snarled at his wolf to hurry when he lapped at her slowly. Christ, she tasted like she smelled. Paradise.

He licked her several times before she came. Luke wanted to take her then, but his wolf wasn't finished. As soon as she came again, this time screaming out her release, his wolf licked her thigh and then sank his teeth into her. Her fingers tightened to the point of pain, but his wolf never let her go.

"Please?" The wolf snarled but held her tightly in his jaws. "What's he doing, Luke? Please tell him to stop. I...it hurts."

Luke commanded his wolf to stop, but he only jerked his head twice. When she cried out again, this time begging him to stop, his wolf backed off. Licking the large wound closed, he let Luke take him. Luke pulled her into his arms while she sobbed on his shoulder.

"I'm so sorry." Luke held her while she cried and told her over and over how sorry he was. Looking down at her leg, he could see the scar already forming and closed his eyes when he saw what he'd done. "He's claimed you as his own. Your human self. I've never...look."

The scar was a perfect outline of his mouth. The bruising was faint now, but he could see where he'd bitten her badly. Luke would bet that if he turned her around, the scar on the other side would be just as perfect as the top mark. He'd only heard of a wolf marking a human like this once before.

"He marked you as his. All the other wolves, wild or were, will know who you belong to and not to touch. Not even Hunter will touch you now, even if I give him permission. He knows to do so would mean his certain death." She asked him why he'd do something like that. "He loves you. He loves you as much as I do."

Luke held her until he felt her body calm. When she stirred in his arms, he looked down at her and smiled. "I guess the mood is ruined now. Tell him the next time he wants to bite me like that to wait until I'm sated. Right now I'm about as sexy as…well, I'm not, am I?"

Instead of answering her, he rocked hard into her heat. His cock was burning to be deep inside of her and she was still very wet. When her ankles wrapped around his hips, Luke held his cock as he moved his crown over her wet entrance.

"I want to fill you slowly and fuck you slower." Her moan had him slide just the tip inside of her. "You're so wet. Christ, I want to fuck you. But I want to go slowly, fuck you like you've teased me."

He slid his crown in again before leaning down and taking her nipple into his mouth. As he nibbled on her, chewing gently on her hardened tip, he lifted her up by her ass and took her to the table. His cock was deep within her, but as soon as he laid her over the table, he pulled out and stared down at her in all her naked glory. Her moan nearly made him enter her again. Instead he pulled a chair to settle between her thighs.

"I'm going to eat you now. Enjoy every drop of your cream, taste you over and over before I fuck you." Jack laid back, and her legs, spread out before him, showed him that she was ready for him to do just as he'd said. As he leaned into her, she put her feet onto his thighs and raised her pussy up to his mouth. Luke suckled her clit into his mouth as he slid his fingers deep within her pussy.

He ate her, devoured her. The more he tasted of her, the more he wanted. His cock hurt so badly now that he had to hold himself. He was sure that any moment he was going to come and he really didn't care. As her legs tightened around his head again, he looked up at her.

If there was anything more beautiful in the world, he would not have believed it. She lay there spent, her body pink from coming so many times, her nipples hard and red from her fingers twisting them, pulling at them as they swayed to and fro from her hard breathing. Standing up, Luke heard the chair crash behind him as she sat up to look at him. He held his cock, fisted it while she looked up at him.

"Fuck me." He nodded and lifted her legs to his shoulders. "Fuck me hard. Fill me, Luke. Fuck me hard enough that I scream until I'm hoarse."

He slid into her. Holding her legs up, he bent her over as he continued to fuck her. She reached for him, pulling his head to hers, and begged him to let her come. Taking her mouth with his, Luke fucked her mouth with his tongue as he did her pussy. Moving in and out of her as quickly as he could until she came again, a short burst of a climax had her sobbing for more.

Letting her legs go, he felt them wrap around him. Moving his mouth down her body to her breast, Luke took the pert nipple into his mouth and sucked hard. As her fingers tightened in his hair, Luke felt his balls fill, tighten against his body until he knew that he was going to come. Lifting his head, he watched her face. Fucking her slowly, bringing her to peak twice more, he held her to him as he poured his seed deep within her. He felt her body squeeze his, milk his cock until he knew that he was going to come again. This time, before he could release deep within her, he licked her shoulder and sank his teeth deep as she screamed out his name, her nails digging deeply as she bit him as hard as he did her. Coming, he felt his wolf race along his skin, never taking him but showing him how pleased he was with their mate. Luke threw back his head when she let go her own howl, and his wolf, always so close to the edge when he took Jack, howled too. He was letting anyone within listening distance know that he'd taken his mate. And Luke knew that he'd found everything he'd ever been looking for in Jack.

~~~

"Sweet and several others are willing to wait for me to get up and running before they sign contracts with me." Jack ate another slice of beef on her cracker. "Did you know that Anderson told them that I had lost my mind and set the fire at my apartment?"

"Did he?" She nodded at Luke but was more focused on filling her belly than what he was doing. "I have someone looking into a few things he's been up to lately. Your man Anderson is going to go belly up soon if things don't change. And since you're going to be opening and taking all his good clients, I think it's a foregone conclusion that he'll fail."

"I don't want anyone to lose their jobs." And she didn't either. While she'd been in the meeting with the clients, Josh had taken several phone calls asking if she was hiring. She had no clue as yet and had Josh tell them that she'd get back to them. "I have a couple of them in mind to help out, but I've no idea how to go about that. Do you?"

"Yes." She put a slice of roast beef in his mouth and watched him chew. "I'm thinking about asking your friend Max to run for the police position. And the Feds have said that they'd help out with things if it got out of control. I think they are imagining bad things to come out of this when all I can see are the possibilities."

Steward had really taken care of everything. The body of Granger had been found in his home with a suicide note. He'd also confessed to taking money from the county he worked for, as well as insurance fraud. Steward had also told them that there were a great many other things he'd done, but that was enough to get others looking into it deeper. There would never be a return on the money, but they at least could breathe easier.

"Max as chief of police? I think he'd do a great job. His wife, Connie, wants to apply for the reception job. Do you think I need one?" Luke laughed and told her she did. "I suppose. Josh is frustrated already about answering the phone. I swear it rings about fifty times an hour."

They finished off the beef and started on the veggies. She would normally love them but since she'd been converted, she didn't care all that much for them. Even Luke seemed to prefer meat over them. She'd have to ask Audra about not cooking them as often.

"I was wondering something." He looked up at her as he massaged her foot. They'd been sitting on the dining room table that had been delivered earlier in the day. She had no idea if it had come put together or Luke had done it by himself, but the sucker was nice. "What are you worth?"

"Are you planning to take out an insurance policy and kill me off?" She laughed when he did and told him she might. "Good to know. But you'll never have to worry about money. I don't."

"Yeah, 'cause you have it." He shook his head. "So you have no money. Good to know too. And how are we affording this house? I'm assuming that the county doesn't pay you that well."

"What I meant was, we have money and a good deal of it, not just me." She frowned, never liking when he talked like this. She was still getting used to being his mate. Talking about how much they had together made her a little uncomfortable. "Jack, what I have is yours; what you have is mine too. We're a couple and we have a great deal of money."

"Why?" When he frowned at her she got off the table and headed to the kitchen. She wasn't worried that he wouldn't follow her, but she needed a minute. When he came in to where she was, he leaned against the doorjamb and watched her. "Why is it our money? I had nothing to do with you making it. And so you know, I didn't ask you that so you'd tell me it was ours. I have a reason that I'll get to in a minute."

"I didn't think you did. And no, you didn't have any say in how I used it or even acquired it. What you did have a part in, and a great deal of it, was making me spend some of it wisely. I wasn't going to buy a house but stay in the pack house for the rest of my days. I didn't buy a new car because I usually shifted and walked everywhere, and you made me think of the future and investing in life. Not just on other ventures but life in general. Since we've been together I've made a great deal of money. All because of you."

He still hadn't moved and she finished loading the dishwasher. Audra was going to be upset with her—she'd told her a million times that she liked cleaning up after them—but Jack was nervous. And when she was nervous, like she was right now, she tended to want to keep her hands busy.

"I will need startup money to make this work." He nodded and continued to stare at her. "A lot. Like nearly ten grand before I can even open my doors."

"I figured four times that, but it's there for you. More actually." She asked him what he meant. "As in, as soon as you tell me the name of your company, the account can be opened."

"And it's all mine to do with as I please for the company." He nodded. "You trust me that much? You trust me with forty grand?"

"I trust you with my life."

She wasn't sure what to say to him about that so said nothing. He stood there for several minutes, what seemed like hours, before he moved toward her. The dishwasher ran quietly behind her as she waited for him to say something to her, like he was joking. Jack had a feeling he wasn't going to, and she found that she was excited about having what she needed to start up the business. She stood very still as he stopped just shy of touching her.

"I put a hundred grand in the bank for you." She looked up at him and started to protest, but he kissed her quiet. "You'll need it until you have your own income. There is payroll to consider, stationary, paints, and other stuff I have no idea of, and other things you'll need as you grow. I want you to do this right. That way when I retire from being mayor, you can support us both."

"I'm terrified." He nodded. "You have that much faith in me? What if I fail from the start? What if…I don't know, I get sued for missing a deadline?"

"You're much too detailed to miss a deadline. And you won't fail simply because you want to make this work. And I hope you're afraid. When you're a little afraid, you'll make sure that every detail is covered, all your contracts are met, and that you work hard for your client. And don't tell me again that you'll fail. Failure is not something you do. You make it work."

"Your dad said the same thing to me when I started to panic at the meeting. He told me I was an Emerson and Emersons did not fail, nor did they act like babies with their thumbs in their mouth when things got tough. I love him for that." Luke nodded. "How did you get so smart? From him?"

"No, my mom. She was the smartest woman I'd ever met when I was younger. She knew just the right thing to say, how to say it and when to say it. She told me when I mentioned I wanted to be an attorney that if I wanted to be a good one then I'd have to make sure that I stayed small enough to satisfy my clients, yet big enough to keep my dream alive. Then I met Slone."

"Slone is scary put together. I've never met a woman who can come into a room and make everyone notice her without saying a word. And she can get you to do things...." Jack shivered. "She's really nice but scary."

"At one time she was as timid and terrified as you are. More so." Jack remembered what she'd read about her as Luke continued. "She's come a very long way in a short amount of time. You and her had a great deal in common, I think."

Jack took it as a compliment to be thought of as her friend. As Luke held her she thought of all the things that were going to happen this week, and she couldn't make herself get all that in a hurry to get things rolling. Being in Luke's arms was like being bathed in the most wondrous warmth.

"I thought you'd like to know that Osborne Construction is out of business. As of this morning. The guys in my office found out all kinds of things the guy was into. I'm pretty sure he's going to be gone for a long time, if not forever. Most of his employees are going to jail as well." She wanted to ask him if anyone had asked about the men that Steward had taken out but didn't. Jack listened as he told her about what things they'd found. "Slone, as the person he stole the most from, will get first dibs on whatever he had. He and his company owe her over ten million in unfulfilled contracts. She's thinking of taking it all and paying what she can to the city for time and trouble."

"I suppose your brother's firm is going to take over the construction projects that were never finished." He said they were already starting on them. "I'm glad. I've been thinking about the library and how much it needs to expand. Slone said that she'd put in for the enlargement of the building several years ago."

"She did. Along with a few other things." He continued to hold her. "I'd like very much to have a child with you. I know you want to wait and so do I, but not too much longer. I was thinking maybe by next Christmas, we could try."

Jack knew nothing of children. She'd never changed a diaper for one, fed it a bottle, nor had she held one. Just thinking about it made her body tense up. But if he noticed, Luke never said a word.

"I guess we can. Maybe we can adopt." He laughed. "I guess we'd have to adopt a cub or something, right?"

"No. We have human babies." She hadn't known that and it took a great deal of pressure off her mind. "I had thought that you'd ask about it instead of letting your mind make up all kinds of things that scared you."

"I have no idea what to ask, much less who to ask." He told her she could ask him anything. "Okay, Mr. Know-it-all. Because I'm not really a wolf, what will our kids be?"

"Children of ours." She liked what he said, but it didn't answer her question. But he continued before she could ask him again. "They might be half wolf and half human, just like you are. But maybe a little more wolf. I don't know. Sometimes a child could be born and be as wolf as their sire. Or sometimes, not often but enough, they can be born as simply human. It's rare but it happens."

"So I have a fifty-fifty chance of just about anything." He laughed and said that was right. She wondered if he really knew or was making shit up as he went along. The man could drive her nuts sometimes.

"Are you going to tell me?" She looked up at him when he spoke. "The name of your company. Are you going to tell me or do I have to wait for the sign to be printed?"

"Oh." She was somewhat embarrassed by the name. She loved it. Jack had thought long and hard on it, but hadn't told anyone yet.

"I thought Howling Advertising." She watched his face. "I have the logo all set up to do. I have to get Hunter's permission, of course, but I'm very tasteful about it."

He still said nothing but stared at her. Jack pulled away and went to the notepad she'd brought in when they'd come down here for a late dinner. Handing him the drawing she'd thought to use, she told him where she'd gotten the idea for the picture.

"You and Hunter were running the other day. I was just coming out of the house and I watched you wrestle around for a bit before you sat down and bayed at the sky. It took me a few seconds to realize that you weren't howling but baying. And at the moon." She ran her finger over the small crescent moon that was just behind the head of the lone wolf. "You gave me so much that I wanted you to be a part of this if I could make it happen."

"It's beautiful." His voice was soft, almost reverent. She wanted to ask him if he'd change it in any way, but she knew that he'd tell her no. Looking at the paper, she wondered if he saw what she'd done. Saw the small cubs, two of them tumbling around in the grass beside him. When she looked up at him, he leaned down and kissed her. Jack had never been loved before and was so glad that, after all this time, she had him as her first and true love.

"I love you." He nodded and picked her up. "Are you going to toss me away? I got news for you. I'll come back at you."

"I'm in love with you too. And I'm going to take you to our room and show you. Several times. All night long." She nodded and smiled at him. "And in the morning, I'm going to marry you. Right there in city hall where anyone who wants to come can join us."

"I'd like that. Very much so." He carried her up the stairs. "And so you know, I already invited Allen."

He stopped moving and looked at her. Then he did the most extraordinary thing. He tossed her over his shoulder and ran up the stairs. She was already wet and ready for him before he threw her onto the bed.

Life was going to be a grand adventure from now on.

About the Author

Kathi Barton, author of the bestselling series Force of Nature, lives in Nashport, Ohio with her husband Paul. In addition to writing full time Kathi likes to spend time with her eight grandkids, three children and three children-in-laws. She writes to relax and have fun.

Her muse, a cross between Jimmy Stewart and Hugh Jackman brings them to life for her readers in a way that has them coming back time and again for more. Her favorite genre is paranormal romance with a great deal of spice. You can visit Kathi on line and drop her an email if you'd like. She loves hearing from her fans. aaronskiss@gmail.com.

Follow Kathi on her blog:
http://kathisbartonauthor.blogspot.com/

www.ingramcontent.com/pod-product-compliance
Lightning Source LLC
Chambersburg PA
CBHW032132170626
46808CB00006B/2206